MON

P9-EDI-726

OCT 1 1 2004

BORDER FEVER

Also by Bill Pronzini
in Large Print:

Boobytrap
Crazybone
Demons
Epitaphs
Firewind
Jackpot
The Vanished
With an Extreme Burning

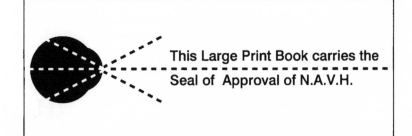

This Large Print Book carries the
Seal of Approval of N.A.V.H.

BORDER FEVER

BILL PRONZINI

JEFF WALLMANN

G.K. Hall & Co. • Waterville, Maine

Published in 2001 by arrangement with
Golden West Literary Agency.

G.K. Hall Large Print Western Series.

The text of this Large Print edition is unabridged.
Other aspects of the book may vary from the original edition.

Set in 16 pt. Plantin by Elena Picard.

Printed in the United States on permanent paper.

Library of Congress Cataloging-in-Publication Data

Pronzini, Bill.
    Border fever / Bill Pronzini and Jeff Wallmann.
      p. cm.
    ISBN 0-7838-9540-2 (lg. print : hc : alk. paper)
    1. Mexican-American Border Region — Fiction.
  2. Revolutionaries — Fiction. 3. Texas Rangers — Fiction.
  4. Mexico — Fiction. 5. Large type books.
  I. Wallmann, Jeffrey M., 1941– II. Title.
  PS3566.R67 B665 2001
  813′.54—dc21
                                               2001026379

BORDER FEVER

ONE

Adobe Junction's largest and finest hotel, *La Hacienda,* was situated in the center of town, not far from the railroad yards on one side and the Mexican quarter on the other. It was a three-story building with an ornate false front, and it provided the softest beds in the territory of Arizona, if the lettering on the sign stretched above its entrance could be believed.

Clement Holmes, who was resting in the iron four-poster in his second-floor room, did not believe the sign at all. "I've slept on rocky hillsides softer than this mattress," he growled.

A distinguished-looking diplomat in his mid-sixties, Holmes was dressed in a flannel nightshirt and a quilted bedjacket; his black Cassimere suit and vest hung in the room's wardrobe. His long silver hair and luxuriant beard gleamed in the dim lamplight which spread across the white coverlet tucked almost to his chin.

His surliness was due not only to the bed. He also was suffering from the grippe, which he had contracted en route to Adobe Junction. It was a minor case, but like a severe cold, had made him grouchy and miserable with a slight fever, bronchial inflammation, catarrhal discharge, and intestinal disorder. And because of its contagiousness, he had been compelled to postpone his plans — indeed, the entire mission — for at least another day.

"I tell you, Captain," Holmes continued, taking a swallow of Dr. Worden's Electric Blackberry Balsam, which the town druggist had assured him was the finest remedy available. "I tell you, except for this damned grippe, I am convinced the worst dangers are over, and we've nothing more to worry about."

"I hope so, sir, but I'd still feel better if you'd let Flynn and Meckleburg stay here in the room with you." Captain Oak M'Candliss of Governor Shannon's special contingent of Territorial Rangers gripped his hat in his hands, nervous and a bit embarrassed by this hitch in plans. Although he couldn't be expected to control Clement Holmes' health, he nonetheless was responsible for the mission's safety and success, now more than ever. "I've got a feeling that something's about to happen."

"Balderdash," Holmes said firmly. "Heartburn, maybe, after that dinner I had." He glanced with a frown toward the tray of dirty dishes. "Worst food south of Tucson, I swear."

"Yes, sir, but the *banditos* —"

"Esteban's renegades wouldn't dare strike here."

"They haven't had any qualms about crossing

8

the border before," M'Candliss protested. "And Esteban has publicly threatened to stop anyone getting in his way, which certainly includes you —"

"Enough," Holmes said, his tone brooking no argument. "Now here, Captain, have one of my cigars, and take a couple to your men. They're both just next door, I've got strong lungs, and the walls are thinner than glass-cloth. They'll have no trouble hearing me if I so much as belch in my sleep."

M'Candliss took the proffered cigars, but he wasn't assured that his assignment to protect Clement Holmes — among others — could not be improved upon. "If you insist, sir. But I won't rest, not until you — all of you — are safely in Prescott."

"Neither will I, if truth be known," Holmes said. "But . . ."

"Sir?"

"It's not only the *banditos* I'm concerned about. If there's to be trouble, it could come from many quarters." Holmes picked up his bottle of patent medicine again, then paused, smiling faintly. "But it won't be tonight, Captain. Not here, and not tonight."

The Ranger went to the door. "I trust not, sir."

M'Candliss went a few feet to the door of the adjoining room, knocked once, and entered. Two burly men looked up from where they were playing pinochle.

"A gift from Mr. Holmes," he said, handing

9

each of them a cigar. "Everything all right in here?"

"It is now, Cap," the one with the beard said.

"Yeah, this sure beats Flynn's chawing tobacco," the other one said. He tore the band off his cigar. "Thanks."

"Thank Mr. Holmes, next time you see him," M'Candliss said. "And there'd better be a next time, so look alive, you two."

"Don't worry, Cap. You going to see Gueterma now?"

"Right. I shouldn't be long."

"You want one of us along?"

M'Candliss shook his head. "There're six in Gueterma's party, and half of them are bodyguards. No, it's our man next door who needs protection, if anyone does." He returned to the door, turning to add: "At least the amount of protection three men can spread over him and seven others."

The door shut behind M'Candliss as he strode along the corridor to the curving staircase that swept down to the lobby. Behind the marble-countered desk, the wizened, chinless clerk paused while stuffing messages in the bank of pigeon-holes and grinned deferentially. "Evening," the clerk said. M'Candliss nodded while passing, pushed through the glass-paned entrance door, and went outside.

M'Candliss cut across the dusty main street and headed south along the boardwalk toward Adobe Junction's premier restaurant, *El*

10

Sacacorchos. As to be expected in a southwestern Arizona town, the restaurant specialized in Mexican dishes, and unlike the hotel, it lived up to its self-proclaimed reputation.

In fact, *El Sacacorchos* was an oasis of elegance in an otherwise crude and often rowdy cowtown. Adobe Junction lay upon a flat crescent of land, the wide, near-empty wash of Pimento River curving around it on one side, with a scattering of trees and a spur of the Southern Pacific on the other. The town was center of the area by virtue of being a railhead, and was the largest settlement between Phileaux Bend and Sonoita, on the border with Mexico — excellent reasons for the converging of gandydancers and gamblers, ranchers and hustlers, cowpokes and drifters into one brawling, hard-drinking melee. Fighting, swearing, dying; they were all in a night's action.

This particular night was still young, it barely being past sunset. The saloons hadn't yet poured sufficient liquor to goad the senses, and most of the regular shops and stores were closed until the morrow. Lancer's Emporium . . . Agave Saloon and Card Room . . . Prinzoni's Barber Shop . . . Wellmenn's Bunks, for those unable to afford the hotel . . . a blacksmith shop, set flush against the livery, across the street from which was the jail made of adobe with iron-barred windows. There were other buildings and signs stretching on down the street, but M'Candliss turned off on the other side of the livery stable, onto a path

11

leading to the porch of a whitewashed adobe building.

The soft gray of dusk silhouetted the hardened features of M'Candliss, an Arizonan by birth and spirit. Raised on a hardscrabble ranch along the San Pedro River, he had learned cattle and tracking from the time he could barely sit a horse. With the wanderlust of youth, he had enlisted in the Fourth Cavalry, serving first as trooper, then scout, and eventually brevet officer, and twice was singled out for special honors because of his reckless bravery and steady nerves while battling the fierce Aravaipas and Pinals. Then, following the massacre of his parents and two elder brothers during a cross-border raid by the Chiricahuas. M'Candliss had resigned to return and run the small homestead and eventually to marry a local rancher's daughter. He had thought of himself as a settled man.

But when his beloved wife, Rachel, had been assaulted and murdered there by a trio of wandering hardcases, M'Candliss had left the ranch, selling out, unable to face the losses it represented. He had applied to the newly-formed Territorial Rangers, and had passed the stringent requirements with ease, for he was an experienced cowpuncher and tracker with a working ability in Spanish, who knew the harsh land and could survive for days on jerky and pinole, and who could shoot swift and straight and be trusted to obey orders. And M'Candliss possessed the necessary motivation: he was determined now to help clean up the Territory, to make it a place where decent men and women could live in peace and security. He was a lonely man, but one tough Ranger.

M'Candliss stepped up to the porch, and *El Sacacorchos'* mustachioed *primero camarero* opened the door and frowned as he surveyed how the Ranger was dressed. M'Candliss ignored the unspoken disapproval, brushing past and heading for the private dining room, which had been reserved for Frederico Gueterma and his party. Tall, lean, his leathery cheeks the color of bronze, his unruly chestnut hair bleached almost blond, M'Candliss was in his workaday garb of flannel shirt, worn leather vest, and faded Levis. The head waiter might not like it, and perhaps some of the more pompous dignitaries might not like it, but as far as M'Candliss was concerned, his assignment was to protect Gueterma, not to ride as part of the Mexican's decorative honor guard. And to his mind that meant he was excused from having to wear such tomfooleries as a starched bosom shirt and pinstriped monkey suit.

He paused by the entrance to the private dining room. Inside, seated at the head of the silver- and china-laden table, was Frederico Gueterma, the special emissary of the President of Mexico, General Porfirio Diaz. Darkly handsome and sporting a trimmed Van Dyke beard, Gueterma had struck M'Candliss as not only a suave and sophisticated diplomat, but as a sharp-witted, entertaining, pleasant companion since their initial meeting

13

that morning in the small border village of Sonoita.

As befitted his station, Gueterma was resplendent in a black silk suit with a diagonal red military stripe running across the breast. A silver medallion hung from his neck, gleaming in the lanternlight filling the private side room of the restaurant.

Six other men, all young junior officers in General Diaz's government, were lined three to either side of Gueterma. They wore dress uniforms heavy with gold braid and carried sidearms in buttoned holsters, and gleaming swords in ornate scabbards. Their faces looked rosily flushed and a little sweaty, either from the heat, their stifling uniforms, or an overindulgence of wine — or, most likely, a combination of all three.

"Ah, *Capitan* M'Candliss," Gueterma said warmly, glancing up from the table. "Come, join us — we were just having dessert."

"Thanks." M'Candliss smiled but shook his head. "I'd better not. I'm not really dressed for the occasion."

"Nonsense. We envy you your comfort, eh, *compadres?*"

And Gueterma's six companions smiled and laughed on cue, while the emissary's brilliant white teeth flashed good-naturedly. M'Candliss' own smile turned tight and ironic. He was a solitary individual, taciturn and fiercely proud, and he bowed to no man, although he respected many. It amused him, yet it made him a little sad, to see

14

these men fawning over the Mexican official.

"I insist," Gueterma continued. He raised the crystal snifter he held in his right hand. "We've had a most excellent repast, *Capitan,* and now a most excellent brandy as well. I insist — if not for dessert, at least for a small libation."

M'Candliss shrugged and crossed to the chair at the end of the table. "You outrank me, so I must oblige," he said as he sat down facing Gueterma. "I do so with pleasure and honor."

"Good, good," Gueterma said. He passed the snifter and an empty glass to M'Candliss. "Now tell me, how is *Señor* Holmes?"

"Better."

"Then we'll be able to travel on to Prescott to-morrow?"

"Can't really tell for sure, not until we see how he's feeling in the morning." M'Candliss sipped his brandy; it was smooth, a refreshing change from the usual rotgut whiskey he drank while out in the field. "If I judge Clement Holmes right, though, he'll insist on going, no matter how sick he is. We might have to rope him in bed."

Gueterma chuckled. "No, it would not do to weary the man."

"It's more than just the problem of trans-porting a sick man," M'Candliss said, becoming serious. "I'm pretty sure he's past the critical stage, but we can't afford the risk of spreading his grippe. There'd be real trouble if, say, you and your men caught it now, on the eve of the conference."

15

Now Gueterma grew somber. "I hadn't considered that."

"Or if the other delegates coming to Prescott came down with it," M'Candliss said. "Clement Holmes is the advance representative of the United States; it would be a major disaster if he proved to be the advance representative of a diplomatic epidemic as well."

"*Qué mala suerte*," Gueterma murmured, frowning.

"Yeah, it would be bad luck if it happened," M'Candliss agreed. "But like I say, I think the danger's past —"

In that moment, with no advance warning whatsoever, the rear and kitchen doors to the dining loom burst open and heavily armed men poured in, surrounding the table. M'Candliss lunged from his chair, his right hand fanning down for the butt of his Colt .45. The Mexican honor guard were also reaching for their weapons, but all of them froze before they had completed their draws. Reason overcame reflex, in the face of cocked and leveled repeating carbines, and a sharp command from one of the intruders:

"Do not move, *señors*, if you value your lives! Hold and be silent before the men of the mighty Ramon Esteban!"

M'Candliss let his hand drop from his holster, slowly straightening as he accepted the futility of the situation. He studied the men who had burst into the room, counting half a dozen of them, most heavily bearded, two in dirty white Mexican

16

peon clothes and the others wearing tattered trail garb. All had bandoliers strung diagonally across their chests, a mockery of Gueterma's proper military stripe, and all wore wide-brimmed sombreros pulled low, shading their faces.

He wondered fleetingly how they had gotten through the kitchen without raising an alarm. Then a moan from that direction gave him his answer. Some of them must have struck the cook and waiter down swiftly and silently, while others massed at the rear door.

"What is the meaning of this?" Gueterma demanded. Unlike his rigidly motionless men, he had scraped back his chair and was rising to his full six feet. Outraged indignation hardened his features. "Leave at once!"

"*Silencio!*" the one who had spoken before snapped. He was short and barrel-chested, and wore a murderous expression. Without turning his head, he barked: "Fernando! Pepe! Take the *Federalista* to the horses."

Immediately, two of the marauders jumped forward and seized Gueterma by the arms. Despite his struggling, he was half dragged, half carried across the floor to the rear door and out into the night beyond.

The honor guard — and M'Candliss — stirred as they watched the abduction. Their hands made no suicidal moves toward their holstered weapons.

The leader of the banditos raised his left hand, holding his Henry .44 rifle steadily with the right.

The remaining three men began to back toward the same rear door through which Gueterma had been taken, their eyes unblinking and malevolent. When they were all a step from the threshold, they seemed to move side by side, almost imperceptibly, as if the maneuver had been prearranged.

"And now, *señors* . . ." the leader began, his lips parting in an ugly parody of a grin that revealed several gold teeth. The Henry rifle rose slightly in his hands.

M'Candliss realized in that instant what was going to happen; realized that the *banditos,* having successfully kidnapped Gueterma, would show those of lesser importance no quarter. They intended to shoot in cold blood, to wipe out the witnesses.

"Look out!" he shouted. "They're going to —"

The rest of his desperate warning was lost in the eruption of four repeating carbines firing simultaneously. The noise in the room was deafening. M'Candliss twisted back away from the table in a flat horizontal dive as bullets screamed and buzzed on all sides of him. Men cried out in agony and bodies spilled across the dining table, sending plates and dishes crashing to the floor.

When he landed on his forearms and thighs he rolled sideways, upending a chair and then slamming into the thick wooden serving table. He groped for one of the table's legs, managed to overturn it and bring it down on top of him. Slugs gouged furrows in its surface as he pulled the table in front of him as a shield. Before he got his body wedged in behind it, a bullet cut a stinging furrow along his left temple. He shook his head, as if flicking away a fly, and dug his Colt from the holster on his hip.

Suddenly — as suddenly as they had appeared — the *banditos* were gone.

M'Candliss raised his head and cautiously peered around the smoke-filled room. It had been a slaughter. The guards were sprawled like ripped and bloodied rag dolls across the shattered remains of the table, food, and fine dinnerware. The walls and polished wood floor were splashed with crimson. The room stank of burnt gunpowder, blood, fear, and death. Only M'Candliss remained alive. It was luck, he knew — that, and having stood instead of remaining in his chair; and having realized what would happen and reacted a second before the actual shooting began.

He scrambled to his feet and ran toward the open rear door. The dead guards had all eternity to wait; he could hear the drumming hoofbeats of the *banditos'* horses in back of the restaurant. His good luck would be their bad luck, he vowed as he ran. They should have killed him while they had the chance, because they weren't going to get another one quite so easily. *They* were the ones who were going to die next, damn them.

Two

M'Candliss hit the steps of the back porch and ran into the middle of the alley between the restaurant and the livery stable. The inches-thick summer dust billowed into a pluming cloud around him, kicked up by the hooves of the horses as the raiders spurred their mounts. The yellowish pall was lung-choking and made the fleeing riders little more than blurred silhouettes that shimmered like objects seen through a sandstorm.

M'Candliss steadied his hand and fired at the retreating shapes. A straggler of the group was having trouble controlling his horse, and M'Candliss directed his second and third shots at him. The man threw up his arms as 255 grains of lead punched a hole through his spine; he slumped forward, beginning to topple. But one heel caught in a stirrup, and he was dragged some twenty yards before his leg finally jarred loose and he dropped at the alley's entrance.

M'Candliss ran. He recognized the fallen man as the one who had smiled just prior to pulling the trigger, obviously pleased at the thought of his bullets striking down the guards. One down, M'Candliss thought as he used his boot to roll the man over and stare at his startled, blood-smeared expression. One down and five to go — plus Gueterma, God help him.

By now, the volley of shots, the abrupt departure of the horsemen, and M'Candliss' return fire had roused the town. Men were tumbling out of the nearby saloons, and a few were dashing from their houses further up the street. They began crowding around M'Candliss as he stood over the body, all of them talking at once.

"What's happened?"

"Where's the sheriff?"

"Somebody get Tucker!"

"Who's the dead man?"

M'Candliss just stood there, not bothering even to try to answer the barrage of questions. A rivulet of blood throbbed from where the *bandito's* bullet had grazed the side of his head, and he daubed the wound with the sleeve of his shirt. He knew he ought to have it looked at, even though it was superficial, but Adobe Junction was without a doctor at the moment; the one they'd had had died recently and a replacement hadn't been found yet. There was a druggist in town, though. M'Candliss could get some sulfa powder from him later on.

A plump, swarthy man with a tarnished badge pinned to a rumpled plaid vest came elbowing his way through the crowd. "What the hell is goin' on here?" he demanded.

21

"You'd better get a posse together, Ed," M'Candliss told him. "Gueterma's been taken by a gang of *banditos.*"

"Hell!" Scowling, Tucker hooked his thumbs into the armholes of his vest. He had large ears and calm eyes, and looked about as dangerous as an old toothless hound. Which was plenty deceptive, M'Candliss knew. Ed Tucker was a shrewd, dedicated, and, when he needed to be, a hardass heller of a lawman.

"Gueterma's honor guard is back there in the restaurant," M'Candliss went on. "What's left of them."

"All dead?"

"Afraid so."

Tucker prodded the dead man on the ground. "This one of the renegades?"

"Yeah. The others got away."

"They head south?"

M'Candliss nodded. "There's still half a chance you can catch up with 'em before they reach the border."

"If that's where they're headed, maybe."

M'Candliss knew that he was thinking of the rumors that the *banditos* had set up a base of operations in the rugged Galiuro Mountains; he'd been thinking the same thing himself. He nodded again. "Or wherever they've decided to take the emissary," he said tersely.

Sheriff Tucker turned to the surrounding men. "You heard enough," he shouted, "so get cracking. I want a dozen of you saddled and armed in the livery yard in ten minutes. Now go on, move!"

Move they did, both townsmen and some of the punchers who had been in the saloons, scattering to collect their mounts and gear. Not all of the bystanders left to join the sheriff's posse — although enough did to fulfill Tucker's arbitrary quota — and those who stayed milled around, talking among themselves, their numbers growing as still more people came and grouped and asked what was going on.

Above their clamor, Tucker's foghorn voice ordered one of them to go fetch his own horse from the stable and a couple of carbines from his office. Then he regarded M'Candliss and asked, "You planning to ride with us?"

M'Candliss shook his head. "I've got to report this."

"To Holmes?"

"Yeah. And can somebody open the telegraph office?"

Before the sheriff could answer, another man pushed forward. He said, his voice harsh and tinged with contempt, "It's them Mexicans again! I keep telling you, they're mad dogs."

"Some are bad, but most are good," Tucker replied coldly. "That's true with any bunch of folk, Arlo, whatever their color or nationality. Stop trying to lump them all together."

"No guts, that's your trouble," the man named Arlo said. "When will you get it through that skull of yours that you can't deal with them? The only thing they understand is a strong dose of rope and lead."

"Arlo," Tucker started to say, "Arlo, listen. You —"

"Rustling our stock, killing our men, raping our women," the man went on, raising his voice. He was big in height, stance, and girth, stretching his denims and flannel shirt with his tensed muscles. His dark leather coat was open, its right side pulled back and tucked against the butt of a S&W .44, his cartridge belt and holster set low on his hip. "Well, by God, they won't get away with it! This is our land now, American land, and we'll band together and hunt them down, till every last —"

"Damn it, Gillette, stop electioneering!" Tucker roared. "You're not campaigning for governor yet!"

"No, but I will," Arlo Gillette retorted. "Somebody has to who isn't afraid to put a halt once and for all to the greasers."

"You're wrong," M'Candliss said evenly. "You're forgetting that the man they swiped was Mexican, one of their own."

"A trick. Probably he was in on it somehow."

"Hell. Fact is, these *banditos* or *revolucionarios* or whatever you want to call this killer gang are as much an enemy of the law-abiding Mexicans as they are of the Americans. The Mexican government's been trying to stamp them out —"

"With an amazing lack of success," Gillette cut in.

"The *banditos* have the run of a thousand square miles of desolate country, and they only strike at widely separated points, with no advance warning. For God's sake, what do you expect?"

"I expect you to show courage, even if the sheriff doesn't," Gillette said. "I can see I had the Rangers pegged wrong too. Well, you've made your point. While you stand around here with your asses pointing the wrong way, my men and I will be doing what should have been done long ago."

"Arlo, we're forming a posse," Tucker said. "If you and your ranch hands are going to ride, you'd best ride with us."

"To hell with you!" Arlo Gillette pivoted and stalked off up the street.

Sighing, Sheriff Tucker led M'Candliss toward the livery yard, where a number of riders were already gathering. "Gillette's a bigoted hothead," Tucker said as they walked. "He owns the Bar-G, the biggest spread 'tween here and the border, and damned if I don't think he knows every one of his steers by name. Just like he knows every gold eagle he ever laid hands on. He loses a yearling, you'd figure it was his left testicle gone."

"Yeah, I can see how worked up he is."

"Well, give him his due; he's lost more'n his share of stock to them raiders, and he's naturally fed up with the rustling and killing. We all are, but still I don't hold with his methods."

"What do you think he'll do?"

"Most likely round up his crew and ride out around the countryside harassing the Mexicans living over here. Christ, they're already scared out of their wits."

"How far will he go?"

"If you mean will he burn 'em out or string 'em up or such like, I doubt it. That'd hurt him politically, and he's got some right fancy notions about running for high office."

"Has he bothered the Mexicans here in town?"

"Not yet," Tucker said. "And he won't, not as long as I'm around. He's got more sense than that."

"But he's liable to stir up others who don't have any sense. If vigilante groups begin riding roughshod, like they did in the South against the Negroes and the Abolitionists . . ."

"Then the Rio Grande's gonna flow blood red." The sheriff shook his head. "But what can I do, Oak? I can't stop Gillette and all the dumb bastards who believe like he does — not one man alone."

"How about gettin' this posse on the trail?" one of the riders said impatiently. "Time's wasting."

"No it's not," Tucker told him. "We're not gonna catch those *banditos* in the dark, no matter what we do. But with the moonlight we got, we'll be able to see their dust miles away out there on the desert, and we'll know which way to head. All we got to do is stay close enough to track 'em come morning."

When the sheriff turned back, M'Candliss

asked him, "Who can open the telegraph office for me?"

"I can," a crabbed, stoop-shouldered man said nearby. "Cable's my name and cabling's my business. My cubbyhole's up the street, by the depot."

"Open up for me, Mr. Cable," M'Candliss told him, "and I'll be along in a few minutes. I've got to stop by the hotel first."

Nodding, Cable hustled toward the rail yards. As he did so, Tucker mounted his horse in response to the growing restiveness of the posse; the grumbling voices of the men filled the night air as heavily as the dust had, thick with resentment and bristling anger. M'Candliss wished them well and then headed for the hotel, hearing the posse gallop off behind him.

Entering *La Hacienda*'s lobby, he saw the hotel clerk sneak a quick drink from a pint bottle of whiskey. When he realized M'Candliss was there, the clerk hastily stashed the bottle under the desk counter. "I was just going off duty," the man explained sheepishly. He cleared his throat. "What was all that hoopla outside? I heard shots."

"I expect you did," M'Candliss said, and left it at that.

The clerk appeared in need of another bracer; his eyes were wide and watery, his mouth crooked in a jittery grin, showing yellowed teeth. "No shooting in here, thank God," he said. "Been right here the whole time and nothing's happened."

M'Candliss passed him by and went upstairs to the second floor. As he approached Clement

Holmes' room, the door next to it popped open. Inside there, Flynn and Meckleburg stood with pistols drawn and leveled.

"Easy," M'Candliss said.

"Sorry, Cap," Flynn said. They holstered their weapons. "Whatever that ruckus was out there really set us on edge."

"It's going to set a lot more than the two of you on edge." M'Candliss knocked on Holmes' door. "Gueterma has been kidnapped."

"What? By who?"

"A half-dozen of Esteban's faithful. They murdered the honor guard and took Gueterma God knows where. Tucker's got a posse out scouring the desert for them now." M'Candliss knocked again, but there was still no response. "Holmes is in there, isn't he?"

Flynn nodded. "Maybe he's just sleeping hard."

"Through all that gunplay?"

"Well, hell, you remember Colonel Dueber, don't you, Cap? The time he drank his way through a saloon brawl when four men were killed? Woke up and said he never heard a thing."

"Never mind Colonel Dueber." M'Candliss rapped louder. Still no answer. "Mr. Holmes!" he called. "Are you in there, sir?"

The silence which followed seemed thick with foreboding. The Rangers frowned at one another, and Meckleburg suggested, "If you want, Cap, I'll go fetch a skeleton key from the desk clerk."

"I don't like this," M'Candliss said. "And I don't want to waste any more time. Break it in."

Meckleburg looked at Flynn; Flynn nodded once. Together they shouldered the door until its lock split from the wood. The two of them tumbled into the room, followed by M'Candliss. Moonlight filtered through an open window; a faint, cool breeze that would die with the coming of dawn rustled the curtains.

"My God!" Flynn gasped. "He's gone!"

M'Candliss walked over to the empty, rumpled bed. "Damn it, this doesn't make sense. Did anyone visit him?"

"Nobody except the clerk," Flynn answered.

Meckleburg said, "Clerk came up a couple of minutes after you left, but that was just to take Mr. Holmes' dinner tray away and deliver another bottle of that snake-oil medicine Mr. Holmes was doctoring himself with. But we were with them the whole time Beasley was in here. That's the clerk's name — Beasley."

M'Candliss nodded. He moved to the bureau, picked up a silver-plated comb and brush set. "All Holmes' things are here; doesn't look like anything has been disturbed. The only thing missing . . ."

"What's missing?" Flynn asked.

"I don't see that bottle of medicine anywhere."

"Say, you're right. That's funny —"

"No funnier than Mr. Holmes sneaking out in his nightclothes," Meckleburg said. "Like magic, I'd say, if I believed in such foolishness."

"We were just next door, Cap," Flynn said. "We should have heard him leave, just like we heard you. This room is the last one on the second floor, and he'd have had to get past ours to get downstairs; the boards squeak no matter how silent you try to be."

M'Candliss stroked his earlobe. "Maybe he didn't go out through the door."

"You mean he went out the window?"

"Could be. You didn't hear anything at all?"

"No, sir, not a sound," Meckleburg said. "And damn it all, Cap, we *were* awake."

"Just like Beasley downstairs," M'Candliss murmured. Yet even if the clerk had been nipping from his whiskey bottle so much he'd been in a stupor, surely Flynn or Meckleburg, so close by, should have responded to any commotion. He regarded his two men. Jay Flynn was the older of the pair, a veteran with the look of long, hard experience about him; Barton Meckleburg was taller and broader, his eyes seeming to sparkle with a certain maverick quality. Both men had always struck M'Candliss as shrewd, competent, and honest. He'd never had reason to doubt their word, and he didn't doubt it now.

But if there hadn't been a commotion, why *hadn't* there been one? Why hadn't Clement Holmes made a sound of any kind?

M'Candliss went to the room's window, which overlooked *La Hacienda*'s side yard. Raising the sash and peering out, he saw a shade-roof below, above the plankboard path that connected the front boardwalk to the hotel's rear stoop. Not an impossible or even a difficult drop to that roof and

30

then to the walkway, but one which would surely have been heard.

As M'Candliss pulled his head back inside, a splinter pricked one of his hands where his fingers were gripping the lower sill on the inside. Glancing at it, he saw a couple of gouges in the wood, but he was unable to attach any significance to the fresh scratch-marks. He looked out the window again, craning his head toward the main street, then frowned in irritation.

"That idiot rancher," he growled.

"Who?" Flynn asked from behind him.

"Arlo Gillette, owner of the Bar-G," M'Candliss explained, his voice tight as he slammed the sash. "He's out there collecting his crew for his own private posse. By the sound of them, he's dragged his men out of most every crib and saloon in town, and they're drunk and belligerent. If he doesn't hold them in tight rein — and I have my doubts that he even wants to — a bunch of Mexicans could die tonight."

M'Candliss stood stolidly in the room, his hands bunched into fists. There was the equivalent of a lynch mob forming out in the main street, under the questionable direction of a reckless man hell-bent for the Territorial governor's seat. And, like Sheriff Tucker, M'Candliss felt frustrated at stopping it.

Jesus, he thought, but his mission had soured mighty fast.

When M'Candliss had originally been given the assignment, he had been told it might involve

31

danger. That was to be expected; that, after all, was what the Arizona Rangers were around to handle. But nobody, not even Governor Jaime Shannon, could have prophesied this.

At the beginning, it had seemed a pretty straightforward matter. M'Candliss, along with two men under his command — he had chosen his top pair, Flynn and Meckleburg — were to accompany Clement Holmes from the Arizona Territorial capital at Prescott to Adobe Junction. Holmes had been picked by Governor Shannon to be an advance representative, sent on ahead of other dignitaries to welcome Frederic Gueterma to American soil. Gueterma, with his combination honor guard and bodyguard, had traveled from Mexico City to represent the Diaz government.

From Adobe Junction, everyone was to ride back to Prescott to attend a special meeting scheduled two days from now. By then, the other delegates would have arrived, including the Lieutenant-Governor of New Mexico Territory, two Senators, and the Secretary of State from Washington, all of these arriving via the newly completed rail line through Texas and New Mexico.

The purpose of the meeting was grim enough without the kind of mess M'Candliss now faced. Potentially, it was one of the grimmest since the Mexican-American War had ended in 1848. The meeting had been arranged in an attempt to thwart an international crisis which, if it got out of hand, could plunge both nations into a war neither one desired.

For the past eight months, the Mexican states of Sonora, Chihuahua, and Coahuila had been all but paralyzed by the forces of a huge band of guerillas dedicated to the overthrow of General Porfirio Diaz's government. These *revolucionarios* were being led by Ramon Esteban, a fanatical follower of the deposed president, Lerdo de Tejada, a politician of great talent and a distinguished liberal who had gained wide popularity through his reforms.

However, Lerdo's haughty manner and intellectual rectitude had soon created powerful enemies, many among his previous supporters, and ultimately he had been unseated by Diaz after the savage Battle of Tecoac in 1876. Since then, Diaz had proven to be a progressive leader, an able administrator, and a promoter of law and order.

Nevertheless, much of the population, especially the peasants in outlying regions, considered Diaz a usurping dictator hardly any better than the loathed Maximilian. Among the dissatisfied had been an ex-peon named Esteban, who had been promoted to a petty official position under Lerdo, then returned to his patch of rock and cactus, lucky to be alive after the slaughterings common to Mexican civil wars. It was this vengeful man whose rallying cry to free Mexico from its alleged tyrannical oppressor had been answered by thousands of disgruntled natives, swelling his band into an awesome army of marauders which Diaz's government seemed unable to control.

Although the United States always kept a concerned eye on political situations south of the border, it normally would not have attempted to interfere in such internal strife. But recent developments, which could not be ignored, had forced the Federal government to act.

Esteban's guerillas, perhaps not commanded personally by him, but evidently under his orders, had invaded United States territory. Over a dozen small villages, plus numerous remote settlements and ranches, had been pillaged and burned, leaving behind looted banks and stores and three dozen murdered men, women, and children. Each time, the survivors reported, the merciless bandits had shouted repeatedly *"Viva Esteban!"* And, more recently, the *banditos* had not fled south, back into Mexico, but north or west into Arizona's desolate Galiuro Mountains. As hard as it was to believe, the evidence was convincing that these Mexican marauders had made a hideout for themselves in the United States.

All along the southwestern extremities of Arizona and New Mexico, American citizens were up in arms. Already one vigilante committee had been formed and had taken reprisal for the *bandito* raids, laying waste a Mexican hamlet and killing five peasants. Dark rumors of other vigilante groups hanging innocent Mexican-Americans were circulating, adding to the ferment. If things were left unchecked — or left to hotheads like Arlo Gillette — a chain reaction of hatred and retaliation could be set off, which would eventually embroil the two countries in major conflict.

President Rutherford B. Hayes had been in communication with General Diaz. It had been decided that representatives from the concerned governments should meet to coordinate some type of strategy aimed at stopping the guerillas and the spread of killings on both sides. It had been hoped that mutual cooperation from the two nations would soothe inflamed passions and allow for peace.

But that had been before now — before this.

Now six Mexican officers were dead; the Mexican representative had been kidnapped; the Arizona representative was missing; and a whole bunch of otherwise reasonable folks were riding around out in the night, ready to blast holes in anybody who spoke Spanish.

And M'Candliss had been charged with keeping things in order.

THREE

M'Candliss returned to the lobby, where a different clerk, short, fat, and bespectacled, was now on duty. Vaguely he remembered the clerk as a face in the crowd which had gathered after the shooting, but just on the off chance the man might know something, M'Candliss paused to ask if he'd been anywhere near the hotel prior to the starting of his shift.

"Nope," the clerk answered, shaking his head. "I was playing pinochle in the Agave up until the gunfight, and then I was out there till the posse left. Fact is, I was dogging your footsteps here, but you were in such a hurry I guess you didn't see me behind you."

"Thanks," M'Candliss said, and went outside. Across the street, in front of the Gilded Possum Casino, Arlo Gillette and his vigilante crew were mounting their horses, preparing to ride. M'Candliss could hear Gillette railing against Mexicans — all Mexicans — and his tirade was frequently punctuated with angry shouts of agreement from his drunken ranch hands. Stonily, M'Candliss kept to his side of the street, ignoring them as he headed for the telegraph office. Before he was halfway there, the riders galloped past him, Gillette in the lead, the image of a righteous avenger.

M'Candliss entered the small office, which was hardly more than a windowless shed adjoining the railway depot. "Sorry I took so long," he told Cable. "It couldn't be helped."

The telegrapher was sitting behind a low, wide desk, looking plainly annoyed. "I was about ready to close up again," he replied sourly. "A feller can't be expected to —"

"I'll make it as quick as possible," M'Candliss said. He placed a U.S. cartwheel on the desk. "Can you raise Prescott?"

"For this, I'll raise hell itself," Cable said. He scooped up the large coin. Then he bent over his key, clicked it with an experienced staccato touch, and a few moments later, the key responded with a rattle of its own. "The line's clear," he said to M'Candliss. "What's your message?"

"It's confidential."

"Every message is, and has been since I started pounding brass," Cable retorted irascibly. "If that ain't good enough for you, then damn your eyes, *you* sit here and send it."

"Mark it confidential," M'Candliss said. "And urgent. To Governor Shannon, Continental Grand Union Hotel. Gueterma kidnapped, Holmes missing and feared same. Advise. M'Candliss."

"Governor, eh?" Cable said.

"That's right. Send it."

Cable hunched over his key again and pounded out the message.

"Now stay put," M'Candliss told him. He gave the telegrapher another cartwheel. "There should be a reply soon and I'll be back for it."

"You're asking a lot, feller."

"I'm paying a lot," M'Candliss answered. "And it's damned important to boot."

He stalked out, went down the street, and stopped at the first saloon he came to. It wasn't a social call, though with all he'd been through, the notion of a drink was tempting. And that curmudgeon of a brass pounder, Cable, hadn't helped his disposition any. But M'Candliss wanted something else saloons abound with — information.

He assumed, as did everyone else, that Esteban's *revolucionarios* were responsible for the kidnap raid; it was what the leader of the group had claimed. He also believed that they must have come from across the border or from the rumored Galiuro Mountain hideout and that they were strangers to Adobe Junction, since no one had been able to identify the man he'd shot by the mouth of the alley.

However, he was aware of one other fact. When he had studied the dead man's face, the thick beard and sun-baked features had not hidden the fact that he was a *norteamericano,* not a Mexican. This bothered M'Candliss, because Esteban sure as hell didn't need any hired help from the States. Or want any, according to all reports.

The contradiction was worth asking about.

38

He discovered little at the first saloon. Nor did he learn anything of importance at the Silver Slipper, the Ace-High, or the Agave. By the time he stepped through the faded batwings of the Buccaneer, he'd talked himself so dry that he ordered a beer.

The bartender was thick-necked and redheaded and spoke with a pronounced Irish brogue. M'Candliss asked him about the raiders as he drew the glass of suds.

" 'Twas a terrible thing that happened," the bartender said as he placed the stein on the bar. "Blackguards, the lot of 'em. And some not even Mexicans, but from here on our side of the fence. Or so I've heard."

M'Candliss leaned forward. "Americans?"

The bartender shrugged. "Some, I suspect. Now I've lived in Adobe Junction ever since good Doc Renault brought me here from Phoenix when I was down on my luck. He's not actually a doctor, truth be known, but was given the label when he opened this establishment. Pitched a tent at first and sold whiskey, women, and Doctor Ricardo Renault's Liniment Balm. That was back before the railroad put its spur in here. I worked as a gandydancer for a time meself, before —"

M'Candliss waved a hand impatiently. He was in no mood to indulge the garrulous maunderings of the bartender; he wanted information. "About the raiders?" he prompted.

"Aye, the raiders." The bartender shrugged again and wiped at the bar with his rag. "Most of 'em are Mexes, y'see, but some ain't. Come a year this August, I recall Darby Boyle passin' through on his way to join up with some brigands somewheres east of here."

"A countryman of yours?"

The bartender flashed M'Candliss an indignant scowl. "Certainly not! Boyle is an Orangeman, and I wouldn't put anything past the likes o' him. Damned if he weren't back within a fortnight, though, sayin' he wasn't gettin' mixed up with no revolutionaries — leastwise, not the Mex kind. The brigands he'd been with was Mexes, y'see. A pack of 'em holed up back in the hills."

"Which hills? Part of the Galiuros?"

"That, Boyle was none too clear about. He said he didn't know where he was most of the time, on account of him being from St. Louis and not a-tall accustomed to our land. Seems like he was also blindfolded when he showed up, bein' a stranger — which added to his confusion, no doubt."

M'Candliss could get nothing more out of the bartender; the episode involving Darby Boyle remained sketchy. Finally, leaving a generous tip, M'Candliss departed the Buccaneer with reservations about the value of what story there was.

Out in the street again, he started up the boardwalk toward the next and last saloon, a drab, mean place called the Bird of Paradise. When he drew abreast of the small alley between the town's bank and the Bird of Paradise, someone called to him out of the darkness.

"*Señor.* Come here, quickly."

M'Candliss paused, peering into the alley. He was unable to see much except a dark figure and, in a random penetration of lanternlight, part of a red-checkered shirt.

"Quickly, *señor*, please!"

"Who're you?" M'Candliss demanded warily, not moving, not liking it. The voice didn't sound particularly Mexican, and though the use of *"señor"* in itself meant little, it was a kind of minor paradox which added to his suspicion. "Show yourself, Mister."

"I can't!" The voice quavered with what seemed to be fear. "They'll kill me if they see me! I beg of you —"

M'Candliss rested the palm of his hand on the butt of his .45, still hesitating while he glanced both ways along the street. There were townsmen and punchers walking along, some of them quite close, but none appeared to be taking any special interest in him. Every instinct warned him that the voice's plea was false, that it was a carefully baited trap.

"Who'll kill you?" he called into the darkness. "Who're *they?*"

"The . . . ones who took Gueterma. I can help you, *señor*, I swear it!"

It was the slight break in the man's hushed voice, the little catch as his attention was momentarily broken by something else . . . something — somebody — behind M'Candliss. M'Candliss pivoted, saw another man loom over him from out of a concealed side doorway to the bank. That one

41

had his arm raised high, and for an instant the pale moonlight filtering in from the street reflected off what he was gripping.

It was a knife — a straight-pointed, double-edged "Arkansas Toothpick." And its razor-keen blade was already plunging toward M'Candliss' chest.

He twisted sharply to his left. He felt the cold steel slide past the corded muscles of his diaphragm, its point nicking his skin as it tore free of his shirt in a wide slashing arc. He brought his left hand hammering up into the man's unprotected face, knew the sound and feel of nose cartilage splitting. The attacker cried out in pain, stumbling to his knees.

M'Candliss swiveled to meet the first man, at the same time kicking out with one foot and catching the falling man in the face with his boot heel. The falling man straightened, his arms windmilling as he sailed out of the alley to plow headfirst across the boardwalk and against a hitching-rail post.

Still pivoting, drawing his revolver, M'Candliss confronted the man who had tried to draw him into the alley. But already that one was backing off, digging out his own pistol. Both men fired simultaneously. The ambusher staggered, pistol slipping from nerveless fingers, and then bumped against the wall of the Bird of Paradise saloon. Both hands came up to claw at his chest, as if he could somehow extract the lead which had cut through him. Then, coughing, he slumped to the alley floor.

Running footsteps retreated behind M'Candliss. Without turning, he knew the second attacker had fled. He holstered his Colt, moved to where the man he had shot slouched against the wall of the saloon, and bent to examine him.

The sound of other running steps interrupted his study. He straightened, glancing back toward the mouth of the alley. Three townsmen came into view, their faces pallid in the moonlight as they hovered by the entrance.

"What's going on in there?"

"Yeah, what were those shots?"

"Bushwhackers," M'Candliss answered grimly as he walked toward the townsmen. "A couple of them; the one lying dead there, and another one who got away. Maybe you spotted him running down the street."

"Was that him? Hell, he bumped into me!" one of the townsmen said. "His face looked like a wagon had rolled over it."

"More of them damned greaser bandits," a second man snapped angrily. A small crowd was gathering now, and there were murmurs of assent. "Something's got to be done about Esteban and his murdering renegades. Maybe Gillette's right; maybe we got to start looking out for our own skins, seeing as the gov'ment don't seem able to do nothing. What do you think, Mister?"

The question was addressed to M'Candliss, the intended victim and therefore the most likely to agree to swift and violent retaliation. And being as he was in nondescript trail garb, he didn't look any different from the other range riders milling around — certainly not like a gov'ment agent. He scrutinized the questioner carefully before answering, setting to memory the man's scruffy, lantern-jawed appearance. Tempers were frayed, and maybe the man was simply quick in his assumptions; but M'Candliss still couldn't help wondering how come he was so fast in blaming Esteban and, by extension, Mexicans in general for the attempted ambush.

"I think we've got to stop the *banditos* all right," M'Candliss replied evenly. "But I also think you'd better go check the man I shot — because he's no more Mexican than we are."

M'Candliss brushed his way through the bystanders and started back down the street toward the telegraph office. He realized it would be worse than useless to try arguing with the man or with any of those who sided with Arlo Gillette's prejudices. The time when mere words could have prevented rash action was now past. Unless something was done, and done soon, to insure the success of the conference in Prescott, the border strip would be whipped into such a fever pitch that there would be no halting further terror and bloodshed. He had to concentrate all his efforts on finding Gueterma and Holmes, and finding them fast.

Entering the small office again, he found the brass pounder playing solitaire on the wide desk. "Your reply came in ten minutes ago," Cable said as he played a red six on a black seven. Still studying his layout, he picked up a piece of paper and handed it across to M'Candliss, then riffled his deck and turned the next card.

The message had been transcribed with a wide-lead pencil:

> *U.S. delegation arriving Prescott noon two days hence. Use any method at your disposal to insure your men there too. Sending rest of your company under command Lieutenant Gordon.*
> *Shannon*

Frowning, M'Candliss reread the message and then folded the paper and put it into his vest pocket. "Thanks, Cable."

The brass pounder was looking for a spot to play. "Sure," he said absently.

"There's an opening for a king," M'Candliss offered.

"I know," Cable said. " 'Cept my deck don't have kings no more. Half the deuces and a tenner are gone too."

M'Candliss left the telegraph office, thinking solitaire wasn't the only way Cable was not playing with a full deck. On the other hand, he himself seemed to be facing what amounted to a stacked deck. He had two days — maybe three, if he stretched it — and that included the time it would take to transport Gueterma and Holmes to Prescott. And he had absolutely no idea where they were, or even if they were still alive.

FOUR

Returning to *La Hacienda,* M'Candliss went up
to the second floor and rapped on the door of the
room belonging to Flynn and Meckleburg. Flynn
answered, and asked him if he had learned anything about Holmes' whereabouts.

"Hell, no," M'Candliss growled. He kicked the
door shut, then tersely briefed his men on the
contents of the telegram, his questioning of the
bartenders, and the attempt on his life.

Meckleburg asked, "You figure Esteban is behind it all?"

"I don't know," M'Candliss replied moodily. "I
honest to God don't, not with all these Americans
cropping up in his supposedly Mexican revolutionary band. I suspect there's a tie-in, though."

"Yeah? How?"

"That's what we've got to find out, and fast."
M'Candliss turned toward the door. "An idea occurred to me on the way here from the telegraph
office. Come on, you can help me."

He went out and down the hall to Holmes'
room. With the lock broken, the door swung open
at his touch; he moved directly to the window,

Flynn and Meckleburg trailing behind him. As he had before, he raised the sash and put his head outside. The main street was noisier than ever, as the saloon and crib trades increased with nightfall. But the walkway beneath M'Candliss, and the rear stoop and yard of the hotel, were deserted, shrouded in deep pockets of shadow.

He turned to glance back at his two men. "I'm going down onto the shade-roof below," he said.

Meckleburg asked, "What for?"

"Because of something I found up here. I'll need a hand coming up again."

"Sure thing, Cap."

M'Candliss swung his legs over the sill and eased downward along the clapboard wall until he was hanging by his fingers. He dropped easily onto the shade-roof. It was a sloping wooden affair, like the gangplank of a ship; it sagged a little under his weight, but held him without cracking.

He hunkered down and studied the rough, dust-covered boarding. In it were scrape marks the same distance apart as the scratches he'd found previously on the window sill. Straightening, he went to the far end of the roof and looked down around the rear corner of the hotel; the back yard stretched on toward a bank of scrub brush, with barren land and rock beyond that.

Satisfied, he returned to the spot beneath the window and was helped back into the room by Flynn and Meckleburg.

"What'd you find out there?" Flynn asked. "Anything important?"

"I think so," M'Candliss said tightly. He pointed out the scratches on the sill, told of the similar scrape marks on the roof boarding. "Way I figure it, the gouges on the roof were made by the legs of a ladder. And the ones here on the sill by hooks nailed to the ladder's top."

"You mean Holmes was snatched out of here by men climbing onto the roof, then laying a ladder to reach up here?"

"It's the only thing that fits," M'Candliss said, and went on to explain. "You know how hot it's been, so it's not surprising for Holmes to have left the window cracked to let air in. It would've been easy for the kidnappers to have hooked their ladder to the sill, climbed up into here, and carried Holmes back down again — all swift and silent, so you wouldn't hear them."

"That don't make sense," Flynn objected. "Even if *we* didn't hear them, Holmes surely would've. Hell, he's a light enough sleeper so he'd have woken up before they got to his bed and gagged him, or hit him over the head, or whatever."

M'Candliss said, "Not if he was drugged first."

"Drugged? But how — ?"

"Didn't one of you tell me earlier that the clerk left a bottle of medicine when he came up?"

"You mean Beasley put something in that bottle?"

"That's just what I mean."

"Hell," Meckleburg said, "it makes sense, at that. I didn't figure the ladder angle because of the lack of noise, but it would work if Holmes was drugged beforehand."

Flynn nodded agreement. "Reckon we ought to have a talk with Beasley, eh, Cap?"

"First thing," M'Candliss said. "Either of you know where we can find him?"

"No. But the clerk on duty now might know.

The three Rangers left the room and hurried downstairs, where they grouped in front of the desk. M'Candliss asked the bespectacled clerk, "Where can we find the gent who was on duty just before you?"

"Beasley?"

"That's right, Beasley."

"Can't I help you instead?"

Meckleburg shook his head. "It's personal."

"I see. Well, he's probably over at the Agave. That's where he usually goes after his shift. He likes his liquor, you see, and he —"

"No, he's not at the Agave," M'Candliss said. "I've checked all the saloons except for the Bird of Paradise."

"Oh, Beasley would never set foot in that place. It's much too rowdy for him."

"Where does he live?"

"Well, it's against hotel policy to give out information like that —"

"To hell with hotel policy," Meckleburg said. He reached across the counter, grasped the clerk by his lapels, and almost dragged him over the top. "If you don't tell us, and damned quick, I'll thump you so hard you'll have to unbutton your fly to blow your nose."

"Shingle-roof house," the clerk stammered. "Picket fence, north edge of town. Please let go — you're hurting me!"

Meckleburg released him. The terrified clerk staggered back against the bank of pigeon-holes, his face flushed and his glasses askew. "The house belongs to Beasley's spinster sister," he said, "b-but she's visiting friends out of town, so Beasley is living there by himself."

"Thanks," M'Candliss said. "We're obliged."

The three of them left the hotel and hurried up the street. Beasley's house proved easy to find. It was, as the clerk had said, a tiny, cottage-like, shingle-roofed house, set back from a neat white picket fence. A tall cottonwood grew in the front yard, and there were prickly pear cactus and flowering shrubs to add color.

The three Rangers had reached the front gate, and M'Candliss had his hand on the latch, when a man's scream split the quiet darkness.

M'Candliss shoved the gate open and raced across the yard, drawing his Colt as he ran. Flynn and Meckleburg were right behind him, their weapons out and ready as well. Another scream came from the house, high and piercing, and then was cut off into a gurgling cry of pain. M'Candliss jumped onto the narrow front porch, braced himself, and slammed his boot against the door near its latch. It had been unlocked and it gave easily, snapping inward to bang off the wall with a sound like a rifle shot.

He went into the house crouching, his Colt extended in front of him. In the neat feminine parlor he saw Vern Beasley slumped against a sideboard — and saw, too, the thick-bodied figure of a second man, the one who had tried to knife him in the alley.

The attacker had straightened and wheeled around, and M'Candliss glimpsed the knife in his hand, the blood coating its long stiletto-like blade. Beasley was holding his stomach, groaning and whimpering; blood oozed out from between his interlocked fingers. But M'Candliss was aware of him only peripherally. His attention was on the man with the knife.

"You again!" the man snarled. Lightning-swift, he reversed the knife with a flip and hurled it at M'Candliss, while with his other hand he cross-drew a Civil War-vintage Remington .44 Army revolver.

M'Candliss had already started to dodge to one side, shouting a warning to Flynn and Meckleburg behind him. The slender blade sailed past his head and stabbed into the wood of the doorjamb, quivering. He angled his Colt to bear and fired. He saw the man's Remington buck as it echoed his shot, but the impact of M'Candliss' bullet in the man's chest half-spun him and sent the answering slug off-target. The bullet from the .44 exploded a porcelain bowl on a shelf to M'Candliss' left, then burrowed harmlessly into the wall. The attacker, slack-jawed, twisted all the way around, staggered, and finally crumpled as

51

his legs gave out beneath him. He landed face up, with blood still pumping out across his shirt front.

M'Candliss kicked the Remington out of the man's limp grip, then bent to look into the ravaged face. The blood stopped pumping as he did so and the eyes went blank; the man was dead. M'Candliss straightened again and went to where Beasley lay.

The hotel clerk was bleeding from a deep stab wound in the abdomen. Fear and pain contorted his chinless face; he knew how badly he was hurt. Whether he lived or died, M'Candliss knew, depended on how promptly he was doctored and how serious the wound was. If the blade had sliced through a vital organ, he wouldn't last long. M'Candliss had seen enough belly wounds to know that.

"No doctor to be had and the sheriff's out with his posse," he muttered to himself. Then, over his shoulder to Flynn, he said, "Find out where the druggist is, Jay, and fetch him."

"Right, Cap." Flynn headed back out the front door.

Meckleburg helped M'Candliss carry the wounded man back into the nearest bedroom, his anguished whimpers trailing off into raspy breathing as he lapsed into unconsciousness. They stretched him out on the coverlet and loosened his clothing. His skin was pale and moist, and he was having difficulty taking air. M'Candliss put pillows under his head and shoulders, covered him with a blanket, then kept watch to make sure he continued to breathe without strangling.

Ten minutes later, Flynn returned with a thin, balding man. "Had some luck," he said. "Found him in his apothecary." He began removing packages of gauze and medicaments from his pockets. "I also picked up what he thought he'd need."

"Listen," the man said diffidently, "I'm not a doctor —"

"You're the closet thing Adobe has to one right now," M'Candliss said.

"But the responsibility —"

"I'll take that, don't worry. You wouldn't have been asked if it wasn't an emergency. This man is the only lead we've got to Esteban and his renegades; we've got to get him patched up at least long enough to talk."

"Well, get out of here while I try." The druggist gestured to Flynn to leave the supplies on the table next to the bed. "But I'm telling you, I refuse to be held responsible."

"Just do your best, that's all."

M'Candliss left the bedroom, Flynn and Meckleburg trailing, and they grouped around the body in the parlor. M'Candliss went through the dead knifer's pockets, and was not surprised by the lack of identification. He did find a pencil stub, cigarette papers and a sack of Dime Durham tobacco, a couple of tokens to a whorehouse in Nogales, and, most important, three hundred dollars in paper currency.

"Blood money," M'Candliss said. "His pay for killing Beasley."

"And you, Cap," Flynn said.

"Yeah — two for the price of one," Meckleburg added. "Well, let's hope he's as unsuccessful with Beasley as he was with you."

M'Candliss nodded. Somberly, the men waited for the druggist to emerge from the bedroom with news about Beasley. An hour passed. M'Candliss began to pace the parlor, his muscles knotted with the need for action, for movement of some kind toward accomplishing his mission. But he knew there was nothing he could do, that he had no direction unless Beasley survived and could tell what he knew.

Finally, the druggist came out, a sheen of sweat on his brow. "Reckon he'll make it," he said wearily. "But he's weak, and infection could set in later."

"Can we talk to him?" M'Candliss asked.

"Not now, I'm afraid. He's still unconscious, and no telling when he'll come to. It'd be dangerous to wake him forcibly."

M'Candliss cursed in frustration.

The druggist left the house, and the three Rangers began taking turns watching Beasley for some sign of returning consciousness. More hours passed; the night seemed to stretch on endlessly. Whenever it wasn't his shift to sit by Beasley's bed, M'Candliss whiled away the time by stalking back and forth, rolling cigarettes, and repeatedly reviewing with Flynn or Meckleburg what little was known or might be deduced.

Then, while Flynn was watching the clerk and the dull gray of an early false dawn was just starting to crease the horizon, Beasley awoke with a high, tormented whine, as if coming out of a nightmare. M'Candliss and Meckleburg rushed into the bedroom. They all gathered around the bed, studying the twitching, frightened, pain-filled man.

"Beasley," M'Candliss said in a low voice. "We're here to help you, Beasley."

"L-leave me alone . . . No, don't . . ."

"Snap out of it. We have to talk to you."

Beasley's eyelids fluttered. "Wh-wha . . . ? You . . . ?"

"Who did it, Beasley? Who knifed you?"

"No! Don't let him . . . !"

"He's dead, he can't hurt you any more. Now who was he? Why'd he do it?"

"I . . . don't know. I never saw him before. But he did it because . . ." The hotel clerk hesitated, as if realizing that to continue would be to talk himself into a prison cell. Yet the attempt on his life had robbed him of all resistance; after a moment, he blurted: "I was to get a hundred dollars for putting laudanum into that elixir bottle and taking it up to Mr. Holmes. A hundred just for that and for keeping my mouth shut, enough money to get me out from under that shrew of a sister of mine. You don't know what that means to me, to get away from her."

"Who arranged the deal with you?"

"Deney . . . Bruno Deney."

"Who's he?"

"Owner of the Galleon silver mine, out in Reñoso Valley, a ways east of here." Beasley coughed, grimaced, but went on. "The mine's played out — never was much good to begin with. I didn't think of it when Deney first came to me, but the Reñoso Valley is nothing but wilderness, and his mine would make a perfect spot to hide somebody."

"D'you know why this Bruno Deney would want to take Holmes?"

"No . . . No, I didn't even know that was what he had in mind when he hired me to dope the bottle. When it happened, it was too late for me to do anything; you understand that, don't you? So I waited here for my money like I was supposed to, only instead of giving me my money, the fellow came and stabbed me." A fever seemed to be burning in Beasley's sick eyes. He struggled to rise, his gnarled fingers clawing at M'Candliss. "But you've got to believe me, I didn't know they were going to grab Mr. Holmes, and I still don't know why they want him."

"Easy," M'Candliss cautioned, forcing Beasley to lie flat. "You've got to rest, get some strength back."

"Y-you're not going to leave me, are you?"

"Sorry, but we've got to. We'll leave word for the druggist to look in on you later on. You won't be alone for very long."

"But that man . . . his friends . . . they might . . ."

"The one out in your parlor won't be bothering anyone except maybe the devil, and his pals are long gone by now." M'Candliss stood from where he'd been sitting on the edge of the bed and frowned down at the hotel clerk. "The only thing you better be praying over is that we get to Holmes and find him alive and unharmed. Your cooperating like this will make it go easier on you, but if Deney or the bunch he's with decide to kill him, you'll be a partner to murder."

Beasley sank lower under the coverlet and began to weep.

The three Rangers wasted no more time. They hurried out of the house and down toward the livery stable, intent on saddling their horses and riding to Reñoso Valley.

Some delay, they knew, would be inevitable, what with having to rouse the hostler, get directions, and leave messages for the druggist and for Sheriff Tucker when he returned. But they were determined to be quick about it, damned quick.

They were literally racing against time.

FIVE

The Rangers topped out on a ridge above Reñoso Valley and reined in their horses. Dawn was two hours past now, and the pale blue of the early-morning sky was being eroded by a heat-shimmering brassiness. It was difficult to focus against the glare, but M'Candliss, squinting, was able to gauge the sunlit vastness of the shattered land below.

Meckleburg spat a stream of tobacco juice. "Down there, eh?"

M'Candliss nodded, stretching his weary muscles. "According to the hostler, Deney's claim would be between here and the valley floor, along with a few others that were staked."

"Too bad he couldn't be more exact," Flynn said. He eyed the narrow trail which wound through the boulders and scrub.

"Well, I figure he did pretty good, considering. These smaller claims must've changed hands and names faster than poker chips at the Agave, and now that they're deserted, it's amazing anybody can remember much of anything about them. Luckily, the Galleon was one of the few fair-to-

58

middlin'-sized mines, so if we just keep to the path, we should come across it and be able to pick it out." M'Candliss rubbed the stubble on his chin. "Best to take it slow, anyway. We want to catch 'em by surprise."

He edged his horse forward. Walked the claybank down the slope, watching for signs of recent activity, of men in the area within the past few days. The others followed. They were unable to find any clue to where Deney's claim might be, until Flynn spotted the butt of a "short-six" cigar. After scouting, Flynn and Meckleburg came upon tracks leading off the narrow trail toward a distant hillock, where mounds of tailings and debris could be seen.

The three men decided to work their way to the mine by moving quietly off the secondary trail and scattering along the hillside, staying under cover and out of sight from both above and below. They made their own trails, weaving through the undergrowth and rock, clawing up steep slopes and easing down declivities where their horses almost slid on their hindquarters.

"We can't go much further on horseback," Flynn told M'Candliss. "Too dangerous — and too noisy, once we get close to the mine entrance."

M'Candliss nodded his agreement, and they all swung out of their saddles. Leading their mounts, they continued to make their way across the desolate land, over brush and around boulders, occasionally sinking leg-deep in soft shale. For a quarter of a mile they wound in and out, always keeping the secondary path within sight. They realized that whatever guards had been posted at the silver mine would be watching the same path and not anticipating an attack from another direction.

Suddenly they came upon a huge gap where a boulder had been dislodged centuries before; it had come crashing down into the valley, leaving a steep but natural pocket. M'Candliss eased up to the rim of the pocket. "It's the mine," he whispered over his shoulder. "I can see the shack down a ways, and a trail going around to where there's the shaft itself."

"Any men?" Flynn asked.

"Two."

Flynn and Meckleburg pushed up to where they could see over the edge of the pocket. In front of them was a gravelly slope which fell away gradually for some twenty-five or thirty yards to the small plank-board shack. Under the roof of the shack, shaded from the glaring sun, were two grizzled-looking men, their rifles leaning against the wall. One was rolling a cigarette and the other had a small pint bottle raised to his lips.

M'Candliss studied the two guards and the surrounding land for a long moment. "There's no way we can get much closer than we are already. We'll have to rush them."

"But, Cap —"

Ignoring Flynn's protest, M'Candliss gripped his Winchester repeater and leaped over the rim.

He plummeted down the slope, risking a fall in his haste, but knowing this was the only way to get a drop on the guards short of shooting them from ambush, which could very well alert and attract their comrades.

"Freeze, you two!" he snapped, leveling his carbine.

Neither of the guards could reach their weapons fast enough, and wisely they didn't try. They straightened, hands raising above their heads, astonishment plain upon their faces.

"Flynn, Meckleburg," M'Candliss called over his shoulder. "Hustle down here and take their irons."

The Rangers carefully slipped over the crest and started toward the guards, staying wide of M'Candliss in case there was trouble. There was, and of a sudden, but it didn't come from the covered men.

Before Flynn or Meckleburg could reach the clearing by the shack, a body of armed men came from around the blind corner leading to the mine shaft itself. They opened fire immediately, a blanket of lead that swirled around M'Candliss and the others, leaving no time for reflection on who they were or why they were there — although, intuitively, M'Candliss knew the answers to both.

He threw himself to one side and returned the fire with his carbine, triggering and levering as fast as he could. On the slope, Flynn had crouched to one knee and Meckleburg had dodged behind an outcropping; both men were firing methodically. The group of outlaws scattered for cover, leaving three dead and a fourth wounded on the trail.

Another went down as M'Candliss squeezed off again, the last shot in his carbine. He drew his Colt and blasted two shots at a big, whiskered man who was taking aim at Flynn. The man buck-jumped backward and slid on his face as he curled forward again. The last of the men in the open darted toward the cover of a boulder, but the earth gave way before he got there and he slid off balance. M'Candliss drew a bead and fired; his bullet ricocheted off the man's belt buckle and tore upward through his chest, sending him sprawling. The fusillade of bullets from Flynn and Meckleburg had the remaining outlaws pinned down. M'Candliss knew that if he was going to make a run for the mine shaft, this would have to be the time.

He scrambled up and made a zigzagging run toward the hill from which the boulder had been ripped. His idea was to go up and over and then to drop down to the shaft. "Cover me!" he shouted as he ran. "I'm going in!"

He reached the steep, dangerous slope. At his first step he sank into loose shale, treacherous as quicksand. He dropped his empty carbine, clawed at the rock with his free hand, and struggled upward even as he felt himself sinking deeper into the shale. His boots found a few solid places, but every inch was a battle which took all his concentration and left him at the mercy of the gunmen below. Bullets snapped around him; scattered fragments of rock stung his face and arms. A part of him expected to be shot with every slow, torturous step he took. But the continual firing of Flynn and Meckleburg helped keep the remaining outlaws pinned down.

Long minutes later, he reached the crest unharmed. He toppled forward on his belly and rolled away from sight. The top of the shale slide was open, windswept, and narrow, but it extended all the way to where he estimated the shaft to be. Cautiously he approached, making a circle above the area as he crawled over the rocky ground. He could see now the crumbling timbers of the supports and the mine shaft's black entrance, near collapse and choked with debris.

M'Candliss eased down from his vantage point on the narrow shelf after first making sure the area was clear of men. He crouched by the mine tunnel to listen; there was no sound from within. He picked up a stone and tossed it inside, then waited a while longer. The rock had hit one wall and caused a dull echo — but that was all.

He gripped his Colt and moved around to step inside. Almost immediately, the tunnel made a turning — the result of the original miners having followed a particular seam of silver. He groped his way around the jog and found that the rest of the tunnel was lit at infrequent intervals by mesquite torches stuck in wall niches. The mesquite provided very poor, faint light, but it was sufficient for M'Candliss to see that the tunnel was nearly caved in, with earth and fallen timbers clogging the passage.

Easing forward, stepping as silently as he could, he picked his way over the solid floor as though it were more loose shale. There was an icy clamminess in the saddle of his back, for he had the distinct sensation that he was not alone in the tunnel. He hoped that the feeling was because he was close now to the kidnapped Clement Holmes; but a part of his mind kept repeating that if Holmes was inside the mine tunnel, there would no doubt be one or more guards present as well.

He crept along, feeling the walls on either side in the murkiness, his boots making small hollow sounds as he moved. Then, ahead, he saw that the tunnel widened into a grotto-like chamber, with still more mesquite torches ringing the enclosed room. He moved closer . . . and saw a length of rope curled in one corner, along with the flannel nightshirt and quilted bedjacket he'd last seen on Clement Holmes.

"What the hell," he muttered. He hurried across the chamber, hunkered to check the abandoned clothing.

"Hold it right there," a hard voice said behind him.

M'Candliss started to turn, to bring his Colt around, but the voice said, "Try it and you're a dead man," and he knew he had no chance to get off a shot before the other man shot him. He froze. And when the voice said, "Drop your gun," he let the Colt slip out of his fingers to clatter on the rock floor.

He turned slowly to face the owner of the voice. In the meager torchlight he was able to make out a short, swarthy man whose black hair grew thick on his temples but became sparse above the eyebrows. A thin strand was brushed sideways across the top of a shiny skull. The man had a Smith & Wesson .44 trained dead center on M'Candliss' chest, and he was mirthlessly smiling, showing white teeth set in very pink gums.

"Bruno Deney." M'Candliss said it as a statement, not as a question.

"That's right," the mine owner acknowledged. He stepped out of the narrow tunnel at the other end of the grotto. "And you'd be one of the Rangers who came in with Holmes. Not that you or the other two outside are going to be any more help to him now than you were before."

"Where is he?"

"Never mind. Get your hands up."

Thin-lipped, M'Candliss did as he was told. "All right," he said. "What've you done with Holmes?"

"Dressed him and sent him on his way." Deney's cold grin broadened. "On *our* way, that is, with a few of my men along to make sure the old boy doesn't get lost."

"What about Gueterma?"

"That Mexican politico?"

"You know who I mean. Did you kidnap him too, bring him here along with Holmes?"

65

That, for some reason, struck Deney as funny; he laughed. "Never mind about Gueterma. Or Holmes. You got plenty enough to worry about as it is." He motioned with his revolver. "Enough palaver. It's time we were moving, unless you'd like to stay here permanently."

"My men are still outside," M'Candliss said. "You can hear the gunfire as well as I can. They'll cut you down as soon as you show yourself."

"We won't be going that way," Deney said. "This tunnel behind me leads clear through to the other side of the mountain. My horse, and some of the others', are waiting back there."

"Then what?"

"Then we ride out of here."

"Where? The Galiuros, maybe?"

"You'll find out when we get there."

"Why do you need me?"

"Because you might come in handy," Deney said. "There's no telling what kind of trouble I might run into along the way, and a hostage like you is an ace in the hole. After we get to where we're going . . ." He let the sentence trail off, shrugging again, but his meaning was obvious.

M'Candliss clenched his fists in helpless anger. There was nothing he could do, unarmed and facing a .44. To try to rush Deney would be suicidal. He would have to bide his time, wait for an opening of some kind.

Deney stepped away from the tunnel opening and went on to say, "Take one of those torches and lead the way through the tunnel. I'll be right

66

behind; if you try anything, I'll shoot you dead."

M'Candliss stepped to the wall and pulled one of the flickering torches free of its niche. As he did so, he noticed that the sporadic gunfire outside had stopped altogether; the battle had evidently ended.

Deney noticed the silence too. "Hurry it up!" he snarled.

M'Candliss started into the tunnel, holding the torch high. It was some five feet wide, with shored rock walls and a low ceiling, so that they had to walk hunched over. Darkness fell away before the advancing torchlight, and the tunnel curved in a long arc through the center of the mountain; it had apparently been built either as an escape route in the event of a mine cave-in, or as a method of quick entrance for its owners approaching from Adobe Junction.

It seemed to M'Candliss that the walk through the tunnel was endless. Their steps echoed hollowly off the rock walls, and dust choked their lungs. And then, all at once, they came around a sharp bend and the oval, partially obstructed mouth of the exit appeared fifty yards distant. Shafts of bright sunlight penetrated the interior.

When they reached the mouth, Deney said, "Walk outside, ten paces. Keep your hands where I can see 'em."

M'Candliss wedged his body past a large boulder that had been rolled up to the mouth to help conceal it, then stepped out onto the rockstrewn mountainside. The hot glare of the desert sun almost blinded him after the dimness of the tunnel. He advanced the ten paces, still holding the burning torch, then turned to wait for Deney, who was just squeezing through the mine opening.

Deney straightened and approached. "The horses are in those outcroppings below."

Blinking, squinting, M'Candliss looked about. "Where?"

"Down there, you blind fool," Deney snapped, turning slightly to indicate the direction. And that was when M'Candliss flung the torch into the man's face.

Deney screamed shrilly as the flaming mesquite seared his eyes, his hair, the flesh of his nose and cheeks. He pawed with his free hand, reflexively squeezing off two wild shots. And then M'Candliss, who had lunged forward the moment the torch left his grip, was on top of the mine owner. Savagely he punched Deney once in the softness of his belly, doubling him over; with his left hand he wrenched the revolver away.

"Stand straight," M'Candliss ordered. He stepped back a number of paces. "You're under arrest."

Deney was gasping, eyebrows and hair singed, skin reddened from the heat of the torch. He was obviously in pain, and staggered while he tried to straighten — but when he came up out of his slouch, he was holding a four-barreled Sharps .32 "stingy gun."

He cut loose with it in that same motion, but

68

M'Candliss hadn't been fooled; he leapt to his right as the little derringer-type pistol blasted at him. Its bullet ricocheted off a boulder inches from his head. He twisted around and returned the fire, but his first shot was too high. He triggered a second and again veered to one side, crouching, as another shot from Deney's vest-pocket hideaway fanned the air near his head. M'Candliss fired a third time, and this one didn't miss. Deney yelled in pain, stumbled back into a sparse growth of scrub, stumbled another few feet, then fell forward on his face.

Cautiously, M'Candliss approached the fallen mine owner. Deney groaned but didn't move; he had dropped the Sharps. M'Candliss kicked the stingy gun away, then bent and used his free hand to turn Deney over. His bullet had struck the man just below the center of the ribcage, and Deney's shirt was sodden with blood, its fabric shredded and blackened around the wound.

"Deney," M'Candliss said, "where's Clement Holmes?"

A crimson froth dribbled from the mine owner's mouth. He wouldn't — or couldn't — speak.

"Damn it, where'd you send Holmes?"

Deney began quivering, arching his back, and gagging.

"Where, Deney? To the Galiuros? With Esteban?" M'Candliss was shouting now. "Is that it? Is Holmes with Esteban?"

Blood flowed out of Deney's nostrils and from

between his lips. He gazed at M'Candliss with waxy eyes, managed a tight, almost cynical grin, and then collapsed, dying with a long sigh.

M'Candliss stood and holstered the .44. He studied the dead man with bleak frustration, then turned and started back toward the tunnel entrance. He was worried about Flynn and Meckleburg, and there was a lot of cleaning up and investigating yet to do before they could return to Adobe Junction. Maybe they'd find out something as to Holmes' destination, but M'Candliss doubted it. Sometimes things worked out simple and straightforward, and other times they didn't; and so far, this was turning out to be one of those times when things didn't — with a vengeance.

"Shit," M'Candliss said, and entered the mine.

Six

Oak M'Candliss was bone-weary as he entered his hotel room, which was directly across the hall from where Holmes had been abducted. He stripped off his soiled, sweaty shirt, filled the washbasin with water from the pitcher, and began a quick cat-wash, preparatory to meeting Flynn and Meckleburg downstairs for lunch. He would have preferred to stretch out on the bed and sleep the day away.

He felt not only physically tired, but mentally drained as well. As he'd feared, they'd found nothing to help them out at the Galleon mine; Bruno Deney had little except personal effects on him, and his henchmen were hardly more than border scum working from order to order, with no knowledge of the whys or whens or wheres. While Meckleburg had remained at the mine to stand guard over the gunhands still alive — neither he nor Flynn had been hurt in the shooting — M'Candliss and Flynn had tried to trace the rest of Deney's gang, the ones who had left earlier with Holmes. It too had proven fruitless; what few tracks there were soon became lost in the stony

71

barrenness of Reñoso Valley. Unequipped for any extended search, the Rangers had been forced to call it off temporarily, and they and their prisoners had returned to Adobe Junction.

Back in town, M'Candliss learned that Sheriff Tucker was still out with his posse. He had jailed Deney's gunnies on his own authority and then notified the druggist to tend to their wounds. Now, as he washed, he dismissed them from his mind and tried to figure what best to do next. His choices were limited, and as far as he could see, the odds lay in gearing up and returning to the mine, where he and his men would start a concerted effort to follow Holmes' trail. And at that, he thought, the odds were poor even if they had plenty of time. As it stood, it was a definite long shot.

M'Candliss took a clean flannel shirt from his bag and was starting to put it on when he heard a soft knocking on his door. "Just a minute," he called, stuffing the shirttails into his pants as he walked to the door. He didn't open it, but stood to one side, drawing his Colt and thumbing back the hammer. "Who is it?"

"*Capitan* M'Candliss?" a tremulous feminine voice said from the hallway outside. "I must speak with you."

M'Candliss frowned, more suspicious than ever. "What is it?"

"Not like this. Please let me in, *Capitan*, it is most urgent, and I have come far. I . . . I am Isabella Gueterma, Frederico Gueterma's daughter. Please, *Capitan* M'Candliss, you must let me in, let me speak with you."

M'Candliss unlatched the door and stepped back, holding his revolver waist-high. He was not about to take chances, especially not with begging young women using important names to gain entry.

The door opened inward a mere foot, and a tall, lithe girl in her early twenties slipped inside, closing the door swiftly behind her.

"Muchas gracias," she said.

M'Candliss stared. He told himself he had never seen her before, yet a part of his mind kept insisting he had. And suddenly his thoughts were flooded with the bleak vision of finding his wife, Rachel, raped and butchered in their sod cabin. He had felt little inclination since then to think of women; but that was different, a man thinking of his wife one way, and of other women other ways — until, abruptly, he faces a woman who reminds him of his wife.

Isabella Gueterma's slender body was as proud and symmetrically proportioned as Rachel's had been. Her dark eyes seemed every bit as huge and dominant, though in a more Latin-featured face. And she wore men's clothing, the way Rachel had; and had the same glistening blue-black hair as Rachel's, worn in the same severely swept-back fashion, although hers was clasped by a beaded drawstring similar to the kind Indians wore. There were differences; there were distinctions. Yet in spite of them, M'Candliss stared at Isabella

Gueterma and saw the reflection of Rachel, night-gown in tatters and soaked crimson with her blood.

It was false, M'Candliss realized, only a dream. But it had been like a dream at the time, a night-mare, with him half out of his mind when he had killed the three drifters who were taking turns mounting his wife. He couldn't damn this woman now for the memories she stirred within him, for having a resemblance that might be mostly in his head, perhaps invisible to anyone else. Perversely, it was almost a relief. Isabella Gueterma was a woman — the first woman he had looked at in a long time.

His face betrayed none of this, and his voice cut harshly into the silence. "*De nada,*" he replied, holstering his revolver. "But if you're *Señor* Gueterma's daughter, what are you doing in Adobe Junction?"

"I have been living in Arizona. Did you not know?"

M'Candliss shook his head, and Isabella went on. "*Si,* I am attending the school in Nogales, to learn English and history and many other subjects which are not taught in Mexico."

"Strange, your father never mentioned you."

"But he must have! He sent me a telegram when he learned that he was being sent to the conference in Prescott. He asked that I leave my school in Nogales and meet him here, so that I might accompany him. He has not seen me in many months, and I . . . I . . ." Isabella burst into

74

tears. "But when I arrived this morning, I hear that my father has been kidnapped by the *revolucionarios,* perhaps murdered." Again she faltered, burying her face in her hands.

M'Candliss felt awkward standing there, as he always did when confronted by a sobbing woman. He didn't know what to do or say, and he certainly had not expected Frederico Gueterma to have a daughter in Arizona Territory, or for her to show up now.

"I'm sorry about your father, *Señorita* Gueterma," he said slowly, unsurely. "But there's every reason to believe he's still alive. If there's a way to get him back safely, we'll find it."

"Oh, *Capitan,* will you save him?"

"Sure," M'Candliss answered, with more conviction than he felt. "Let me just finish here, and we'll go down to the café and have something to eat. My men are probably there already, and you'll see we're all dedicated to tracking down those *banditos* and saving your father before they can harm him."

As he spoke, M'Candliss turned to take his vest from the back of the room's chair. He failed to see the young woman's face suddenly lose its tormented expression and become grimly determined. He failed to see the swift movement with which she drew a smallish .38 Colt "Lightning" pistol from a concealed holster in her denims. And he failed to see her take two quick, silent steps forward, matching the twin strides he had taken toward his chair, and raise the pistol high

75

over her head. All M'Candliss knew was an abrupt, blinding explosion of pain as the pistol barrel collided with his skull. Brilliant white light flashed in back of his eyes, then winked out into total blackness . . .

There was sunlight glaring down at him.

M'Candliss sensed the blistering heat first as consciousness gradually returned. But the sun was not overhead, or the heat would be searing his eyelids; it was off to one side. Mid-afternoon, or perhaps a little later. The sensation of thirst came to him, and he was aware of a parched, dusty taste in his mouth. He opened his eyes, his thoughts still jumbled and ravaged by pain.

Through his slitted lids, he saw the hot blue expanse of sky overhead. When he turned his head the blue became flaked with gold, then turned into a pale yellow, then into the searing white of the sun. He turned his head back the other way and closed his eyes again.

Then he realized that he was moving. He listened: a squeaky axle on one side, the dull rumbling of three other wheels, the padding of horses' hooves and the occasional jingle of harness and collar. Wagon. He was lying on his back in the bed of a wagon.

He tried to move, and couldn't. And another realization came to him: he was trussed up with rope. His arms and legs were numb from the lack of circulation. He couldn't even speak; he was gagged with his own neckerchief. There was a shadow over his face, and when he opened his eyes again to see why, he found himself looking up into the black pools of Isabella Gueterma's eyes. She was bending over him, one hand cradling his head, the other hand holding a canteen.

"Capitan?" There was concern in her voice. *"Capitan?"*

M'Candliss managed a weak nod.

"Bueno, you are awake at last. Listen to me, *Capitan,* I will take off your gag so you may drink, but please do not be so foolish as to think I will remove your ropes, or that you can escape. My father will be ready and promises to shoot. *Entiende?"*

M'Candliss nodded that he understood, but he did not. Father? Isabella's father, Frederico Gueterma? M'Candliss' head cleared with the impact of her words. He struggled to sit up, the girl helping him, leaning forward, and untying his kerchief.

She held the canteen to his parched lips, and M'Candliss drank slowly, making sure his lips were wet and the inside of his mouth satiated before swallowing. He managed to say, "Your father?"

"Si," she said, nodding. *"Mi padre. Por qué?"*

Why indeed, M'Candliss thought. He twisted about so he could see the man she was calling father. The wagon was a narrow-track, stiff-tongued, standard open farm type, very old and lacking paint. The man was straddling the spring seat so that he could handle the reins and keep an eye on his prisoner. There was a .56 Spencer held by one leg against the seat, and that big Spencer could bore a hole through him easily. The man was slim, small, a dark-skinned Mexican, and not at all like Frederico Gueterma.

The man glowered at M'Candliss. M'Candliss turned back to the girl. "He's your father, is he?"

The girl, realizing his confusion, smiled and nodded. "I lied, *Capitan. Señor* Gueterma is not of my blood. I am Isabella Ortiz, and there is my true *padre*, Alfredo Ortiz."

Alfredo Ortiz said nothing. His expression was enough: contempt, resentment, a little fear.

M'Candliss turned away from both girl and man for a moment and stared out at the landscape. It was the rugged country of the Southwest canyons, brush, boulders, and sand — an endless desert sparsely grown with prickly pear, barrel cactus, huisache, and scarlet-streaming octillo. Ahead were the silent, forbidding steppes leading to the Galiuro Mountains, which rose in a series of spires, plateaus, and cragged canyons.

Tied to the back of the wagon was M'Candliss' claybank gelding. He turned back to the girl. "Why'd you bring my horse along?"

"Ah, but of course we would. Would it not seem strange if your men found you missing but not your horse? This way, they will think you are out on an errand, perhaps, and will not worry."

"They'll never fall for that."

"Perhaps. You know your men better than we do. But it was worth a try, *verdad?*" Isabella adjusted the chin strap of the wide sombrero she now wore. Her father also wore a large hat, though narrower of brim and more tattered.

M'Candliss ran his hand through his hair, wincing as he touched the tender spot where she had gun-whipped him, and wished that the girl had thought to bring along his own hat instead of his horse. He said, "Okay, so where are you taking me?"

Isabella looked at her father, then back at M'Candliss, and averted her eyes as she had back in the hotel room, as if embarrassed. Alfredo Ortiz answered for her. "There," he said, pointing toward the Galiuros. "To the camp of the *revolucionarios*. My people."

"Is that where Gueterma was taken last night?"

Isabella shrugged; if she knew, she wasn't telling.

M'Candliss demanded angrily, "Why have your people, as you call them, crossed the border to kill and plunder us?"

The father spat over the side of the wagon, an expansive gesture of scorn in a land of little water. "Listen to the gringo! All gringos have grown soft since their *revolucion*. What does he know of our struggle, eh? Nothing."

"I know your fight is a Mexican one, not an American one," M'Candliss snapped. "Whatever we are is no excuse for your actions."

"Excuse? *Oiga!*" Isabella said. "We fight for our lives, for our families, for our freedom, for our rights as human beings. We must conquer the *federalistas,* but we are so few against their many. We have been forced to be dishonorable at times, but is it not better to soil the hands so that one may have the chance of washing the whole body later?"

M'Candliss fell silent. Isabella and Alfredo Ortiz were obviously visionary and idealistic. Sincere, perhaps, but grim with the necessity of their mission. Were the revolutionaries really banded together for freedom, or just for the sheer hell of it?

Isabella seemed to need to talk more. "The *federalistas, Capitan* M'Candliss, the soldiers such as were shot in Adobe Junction, killed my mother. Murdered her after . . . using her." The girl squeezed her eyes shut. "I do not pity the ones who died yesterday."

"Isabella," Alfredo Ortiz warned, "we were told not to speak to this *hombre.* It is against my judgement even to allow the gringo the comfort of water."

"I am sorry I deceived you, *Capitan,*" Isabella said, in defiance of her father. "I am sorry for you and for all of us."

"Why have I been taken, Isabella?"

She shook her head. "I follow orders. I do not know."

"*Silencio!*" Ortiz grabbed the stock of the Spencer for emphasis.

They crossed arroyos and dry stream beds, entered apparently dead-end box canyons but always managed to find their way through. They moved forward and upward, into wilderness and isolation.

Hours dragged by until, as dusk was darkening into late evening, a voice called out from a shadowed ledge, *"Quien vive?"*

Ortiz reined the horses and raised his hands to his mouth.

"El Grito!" The Insurrection.

"Entra."

Ortiz gave a flip of the reins on the team's withers, and the wagon lurched forward. A hundred yards more and all trace of the sentry was gone. M'Candliss reflected on what an easy place this was to live or die. No one would be aware of either.

There was one bend after another, one sharp dip or rise followed by still more curves. The air grew cool; one horse whinnied, scenting water. Then there was a narrow cleft where the bottom was almost a tunnel between the towering cliff faces, and after passing through, M'Candliss saw that they were on the wall of a vast depression, shaped like a huge bowl, that dipped down and around.

He heard a trickle of water in the near-distant gloom — a small waterfall which splashed into a pool of worn rock, then snaked its way into the bowl. Around the water grew sparse grass, and where it collected in the bottom of the bowl were a few scraggly cottonwoods and cedars. The desert mountains were like this, concealing canyons until one stood on their very edge.

They descended, heading toward a ring of small campfires that were close by the trees. This, M'Candliss realized, must be the fortress that Darby Boyle had reported to the Buccaneer's bartender. A natural fort which could be defended against the most intense attack with ease, this would be a perfect encampment for outlaws or *revolucionarios.*

The Mexican rebels were badly equipped, which didn't surprise M'Candliss. There weren't any adobes or massive placements, or even a crude perimeter of stakes. The harsh mountains ringing them would serve as protection enough.

Perhaps a hundred men were around the campfires. Rifles were stacked, equipment scattered. Horses and mules stood with their *aparejos* in place; a few dogs slept or fought over scraps.

Whatever else the *revolucionarios* were, they were not military minded. The men rose and crowded around the wagon, a coarse and swarthy lot, sporting bandoliers and "Prairie" cartridge belts. Some were straw-hatted, but all stared and made crude comments openly and loudly. M'Candliss had seen their type before on both sides of the border, clean-shaven or whiskered, fancy-dressed or in tatters. These men were not peasants driven to extremes by oppression, by tyrants — they were oppressive tyrants themselves. Killers and thugs without morals or scruples, they would, if they ever gained control, be as corrupt and evil as the rulers they supplanted.

M'Candliss glanced back at Isabella and her father. They did not belong here, blinded as they were by their zeal. The *señorita* had said she was sorry; but now, seeing the glinting eyes, the razored knives and low-slung sidearms of the so-called revolutionaries, M'Candliss felt sorry for her and Alfredo Ortiz. The Ortiz family was being used in an immoral war. Their deaths would be empty and in vain.

He couldn't help wondering how many other decent yet naive patriots were being similarly duped. Not that Ramon Esteban's uprising was in itself necessarily unjust or false, he realized; it could be that this particular gang was merely an outlying extension of the main rebel force, one which Esteban would not sanction if he knew its contents and the makeup of its members. After all, the State of Chihuahua, where Esteban mainly rode, was a long way off. On the other hand, Esteban might well be aware and either didn't care and was no better than these men, or was suffering them for lack of the power to disband them. It could even be that this was a rival band of insurrectionists, one not dedicated like the Ortizes and Esteban to a crusade for freedom from oppression, but using the call to liberty as a license to plunder and murder.

It troubled M'Candliss not to have some idea of an answer. What he did and his chances of staying alive depended on knowing what he was up against — and at this point, his best guess was that he'd soon be up against a wall, facing a firing squad.

The wagon stopped in front of the largest of three tents. This would be the headquarters of the leader, the one who had commanded the attack on the restaurant, the kidnapping of Gueterma, and the ambush of M'Candliss in the alley. And quite possibly had been the brains behind Bruno Deney's snatching of Clement Holmes, which could mean, M'Candliss hoped, that Holmes was alive and being held in this camp too.

He tensed expectantly, straining against his bonds as Alfredo Ortiz jumped down from the seat and went up to the man guarding the tent flap. The guard turned and ducked under the flap. He was gone but a moment, returning with the leader of the camp.

The leader — this *Gran Géneral de La Revolucion* — strode to the wagon bed and stared up at M'Candliss. He was dressed similarly to his men, though in a slightly better pair of boots, a newer, less stained shirt, and a pair of pants without holes. Around his waist were two cartridge belts and holsters, one of brown leather and one of black and with differing designs, but the *pistolas* he carried were both pearl-handled.

"*Buenas tardes, Capitan* M'Candliss!" he said with a grin.

The man was Frederico Gueterma.

SEVEN

M'Candliss stared at the handsome countenance of the Mexican emissary. Gueterma responded with a cold smile, eyeing M'Candliss as he might a steer in a slaughter pen.

"Have you nothing to say, *Capitan?*" Gueterma asked. "I had expected more reaction than outraged silence."

"I can't believe that a man lives who could sit eating and drinking and joking with his own loyal guards, knowing he's sentenced them to be butchered," M'Candliss replied with tight-lipped fury.

"Loyal? Pigs!" Gueterma spat. "Pawns of Diaz and his *Federalistas!* They deserved no mercy; they deserved only to die."

"Is this the sort of man you want to lead your people?" M'Candliss said, turning to the Ortizes. "A cold-blooded killer who surrounds himself with cut-throat bandits?"

Isabella seemed to flinch, but then her expression set with grim determination. Alfredo Ortiz remained stoic, his head held high and proud. But M'Candliss' words had a definite effect on Gueterma. Rage blotched his features, and he

85

leaned forward to slap the defenseless Ranger once, twice, three times.

M'Candliss took the blows without wincing, his eyes fastened on the Mexican traitor's face, sparking with frustration and hatred. Gueterma had personally supervised the wanton massacre of almost half a hundred innocent people in the past few months. That was plainly evident now, as was the power-mad compulsion which controlled him.

"Untie this *cretino* and bring him to the fire," Gueterma said to the guard beside him. "I wish to tell him some things in privacy."

The guard, aided by Alfredo, loosened the ropes binding M'Candliss, then pulled him out of the wagon and half dragged him toward the nearest campfire, where he threw him roughly to the ground. Gueterma came striding over, the dancing flames from the bonfire making his face look like the mask of some grinning demon. The guard hastened back into the tent; an instant later, he reappeared with a folding stool. Gueterma sat down on it a few feet away from M'Candliss, and impatiently waved away the guard.

Watching all this, M'Candliss noticed that Isabella and her father lingered closer than the guard or the other members of the gang, huddling around the embers of a smaller, dying fire some twenty yards away. Isabella, avoiding M'Candliss' gaze, began to rekindle the fire. M'Candliss turned his attention back to Gueterma, licking his parched lips as he saw Gueterma light a thin cheroot with a piece of kindling.

"Why did you have me brought here?" M'Candliss asked in a hoarse voice. "You tried to have me killed twice last night, and now you have had me kidnapped instead. Why, Gueterma?"

"For good reason, *Capitan*," Gueterma said. "I did not think of this until I had ordered you disposed of, but I am glad now that the attempts on your life failed. You are much more valuable alive."

"For the moment, I suppose?"

"*Sí,* for the moment."

"That still doesn't answer why."

"You'll learn, in due course."

"Does Esteban know of this, of what you've done?"

"Ramon Esteban is a *baboso* — a fool."

"In other words, he doesn't know what you're up to. Yeah, that figures. According to *Señorita* Ortiz, you're a part of Esteban's *grito,* but from what I've heard about Esteban, he wouldn't condone the kind of indiscriminate killing and looting you've been doing."

"Astute of you, *Capitan* — more astute than Esteban has been. He believes me to be on his side, that I am backing his rise to the Presidency of Mexico by helping him overthrow Diaz's government. But in reality, it is *I* who will become *El Presidente.*" Gueterma leaned forward, pointing his cheroot at M'Candliss like a spear. "My men here, and others like them in New Mexico, and mixed with Esteban's *revolucionarios* in Chi-

87

huahua, will see to it that Esteban and his loyalists are properly taken care of when the time comes."

M'Candliss was beginning to understand. "So that's why you're raiding on this side of the border. You *want* retaliation, vigilante committees lynching innocent men, reprisal raids into Mexico. You *want* hatred to grow between our countries — so there'll be war."

"But of course! Such a war could only weaken Diaz's government and make it easier for Esteban and his *grito* to succeed."

"I suppose the kidnapping of Clement Holmes is part of it too. What do you plan to do? Kill him and make it look like Esteban was responsible? Or have you already killed him?"

"*Señor* Holmes is not dead," Gueterma said. "Not yet. But yes, his eventual death is part of my plan."

"Where is he? Have you got him here?"

"No, he is not here. But you should not concern yourself with his whereabouts, *Capitan*. There is nothing you can do to help him. Or to help anyone else — including yourself."

M'Candliss held his rage in tight check. He said, "I don't see the reasoning behind your own kidnapping last night. That and the shooting of your honor guard will help stir up bad feeling, yes; but if this bunch here is supposed to be part of Esteban's revolutionaries, how are you going to explain riding into Mexico later on as their leader?"

"There will be no need for explanations,"

Gueterma said. "At the proper time, I will pretend to escape from this band and join Esteban's main force in Chihuahua. When I am asked I shall say that these men were renegades, unaffiliated with the noble *grito,* and I will denounce their activities."

"You have everything figured, don't you?"

"Yes, *Capitan,* I do have everything figured. The Mexican people, once war breaks out, will flock to Esteban, for he is one of their own and they will be fearful, disgruntled, and be eagerly receptive to his promises for change and prosperity."

"And peace," M'Candliss added bitterly. "Then, once the overthrow is complete, some fatal accident will happen to Esteban."

"A national tragedy. But I'll be there to step in before my country can lose yet another war with your country. Not Esteban but I will be the one who will sue for peace, and it will establish me as a wise and benevolent leader in the eyes of both our peoples."

"And the whole time you're being hailed as the savior of Mexico, you and your gunhands will be robbing it blind."

Gueterma laughed. "Even if you're right, no one will know of it or be able to do anything about it. I will be too firmly in power. The name of Frederico Gueterma will be on the lips of every citizen, shouted in the streets and blessed in every prayer."

"Not if I can stop you."

"Ah, the irony! You will not stop me, my dear

Capitan — you will help me. You will be a key figure in one of the final two incidents which will ignite the war. In a couple of days, an important official in Diaz's government will be assassinated, a man who opposed my appointment as emissary to the meeting in Prescott. You will be there too, at the capital, and will be blamed for his death."

"You're crazy! Nobody'd believe I would murder a Mexican official."

"But they will. We'll be taking you to Mexico City, but it will appear as if that was your destination when you left Adobe Junction on your own. And it will be rumored that you turned assassin to avenge the deaths of the United States Senators and the Secretary of State."

"What? What are you talking about?"

"The train carrying the delegates to the conference in Prescott will be blown up as it crosses the trestle at Saddleback Gorge," Gueterma said with relish. "My men and I will be there to make sure there are no survivors of the explosion."

M'Candliss was shocked speechless. Gueterma's intentions were the most depraved he had ever heard, for he knew the territory where Saddleback Gorge was located. More than a day's ride from this Galiuro fortress, the gorge was in the remote, formidable Dos Cabezas Mountains, a range the railroad had found to be almost impenetrable. The section was treacherous at best, and if Gueterma and his gang dynamited the spindly trestle just as the train crossed over it, not a passenger on board would escape death.

M'Candliss looked past Gueterma and saw that Alfredo Ortiz had left the other fire, where Isabella appeared to be preparing a meal, and had edged closer to where M'Candliss and Gueterma were. Perhaps he was curious about the conversation, M'Candliss thought; he and Gueterma had been speaking in anything but soft voices.

An idea came to him. If he could keep Gueterma talking, make him reveal the kind of madman he was while Alfredo Ortiz was within earshot, it might be enough to jar the old man into reacting. As loyal to Mexico as Ortiz seemed to be, he might rashly break in, confront Gueterma, or even try to struggle with him. If he caused enough of an uproar, the diversion might allow M'Candliss the chance to get away.

Away to where, though? Assuming he had the luck to escape the camp itself, M'Candliss doubted he'd have enough time to grab a horse, much less a weapon to use, and he had no idea where in the Galiuros he was. He'd be pursued by shrewd, experienced hunters, and should he somehow manage to elude them, he'd still have to cross a rocky, arid wasteland before he could reach help.

Yet he knew he had to try. And if this failed, as it most likely would, then he must try again and again. Once they broke camp, each minute would send him that much farther away, as Gueterma took him south to Mexico City and a rendezvous with murder. M'Candliss held no illusions what would happen to him there. He'd be shot down

91

near the point of the assassination, and the rifle which killed the Mexican official would be discovered in his hands. And a great many others of both nationalities would also die.

M'Candliss waited until Ortiz had edged to within a few feet of them, standing almost directly behind Gueterma. Then he asked, "What's going to happen to Esteban? I mean, I imagine you'll rig a convenient accident for him, but what exactly did you have in mind? Another train wreck like the one you're planning for the delegates?"

Gueterma's eyes flashed in the firelight. "He will be struck down by the bullet of a *Federalista,* of course, thus cementing my position and my politics with the people. Esteban will become a martyr, a dead and mourned martyr — and there is nothing better with which to strengthen any cause."

M'Candliss saw Alfredo Ortiz stop as if frozen. Only a few feet from Gueterma, Ortiz had overheard the exchange, and his face was etched with shock. He stared at Gueterma's broad back with unblinking eyes.

"Gold and power, those are your twin causes, Gueterma," M'Candliss snapped. "You care nothing for your people, for their well-being and liberty."

"If it so pleases you, *Capitan,* it is true. I have only contempt for the brainless peons. But it is they who will cry '*Viva* Gueterma!', who will bow at my passage, who will do my every bidding. They beg to be used — so they will be."

"Just as you're using Alfredo and Isabella Ortiz?" M'Candliss said. "Just like you're taking them in, is that it?"

"*Si!* They are like Esteban, blinded by their own witless patriotism —"

A bellow of rage erupted from behind Gueterma, and Alfredo Ortiz hurtled forward. His features were contorted, his gnarled peasant's hands bunched into fists.

Gueterma swung around at the shout, then struggled to his feet, upsetting his stool as he saw Ortiz rushing toward him.

"Traitor!" Ortiz yelled at him, his hands punching and clawing. "Filthy *guarro!* You have deceived us all along! The gringo was right! I kill you with my bare hands!"

Gueterma swung an elbow viciously into the old man's ribs, sending him staggering backward to sprawl in the dust. Then Gueterma drew one of the pearl-handed revolvers at his side and shot Ortiz in the chest while the old man was squirming helpless on the ground.

Isabella screamed in horror from the other campfire, dropping the pan in which she had been cooking scraps of meat. *"Madre de Dios! Padre!"*

Alfredo Ortiz grunted once, painfully. Gueterma shot him a second time, and Ortiz twitched, then lay still.

Isabella ran to her father and flung herself down beside him. She cradled him to her breast, her soft hair covering both of them like a shroud, and she cried abjectly, *"Padre . . . Padre . . ."*

M'Candliss felt sick at the brutal sight he had just witnessed. When he had conceived the idea to pit Ortiz against Gueterma, it hadn't occurred to him that Gueterma would slaughter the unarmed old man. It was his fault Ortiz had died as he had, even though his death as a revolutionary was almost inevitable.

Gueterma holstered his revolver. "I am sorry, *señorita*," he said to Isabella, "but your father became deranged and attacked me. I was forced to defend myself, as you must have seen."

She did not answer him. She was moaning softly, holding the dead body of her father.

M'Candliss said, "Yeah, you must've seen, Isabella. You must've seen the kind of inhuman animal Gueterma is. He murdered your father in cold blood!"

"Enough, *Capitan*," Gueterma told him. "The girl knows I acted in self-defense, that I would not have killed her father if he had not lost his head and attacked me. But he will not have died in vain. *El grito* will triumph!"

M'Candliss held his tongue. He did not want to have the girl killed too. A long silence ensued. Isabella lowered the body of her father down to the ground, then stood and stared dry-eyed at M'Candliss and Gueterma. There was a spark of defiance, of hatred, in her eyes.

"My leader is right, gringo," she said to M'Candliss. "I do not condemn him for doing what he had to do; my father was old and perhaps the strain became too great for his mind. He has died so that others may gain their freedom." She glanced down at her father. "Any price is worth the salvation of my people. *Any* price."

M'Candliss felt a sinking sensation in the pit of his stomach. He slumped backwards, weary. All hope seemed gone now of ever getting out of this camp alive, of saving the lives of the delegates on board the train, of stopping two nations from going to war.

EIGHT

Gueterma had nothing more to say to either M'Candliss or the woman. Instead he put his back to them and spoke to a group of men who had gathered around. "Begin loading the wagons," he told them. "We must leave at once, *caballeros*, for Saddleback Gorge."

There was a flurry of activity. Two wagons were rolled over to where a canvas tarpaulin covered several wooden crates. These were lifted into the wagons and tied down carefully. M'Candliss saw that roughly half the camp, about fifty men, were to be at the scene of the ambush in Saddleback Gorge. Gueterma was taking no chances, with half a hundred men and two wagonloads of explosives, of anyone aboard the delegates' train escaping with their lives.

Isabella Ortiz had got two of the *banditos* to carry her father's body to the bank of the pond, where they laid him, wrapped in a blanket, for burial. M'Candliss heard the men tell her that they would dig a grave later, after Gueterma and the others had left camp.

M'Candliss wondered how any woman could

be so zealous in her beliefs as to venerate her father's killer. Perhaps she would break down later — but later would be too late. Now she sat alone by the little fire, cooking the supper which had been intended for two and was now for one, her lips taut and her face a mask. She might have been made of stone.

She did not look up as Gueterma, astride his horse, ordered the formation of two columns of *banditos* with the wagons between them. Gueterma called out in Spanish for the columns to proceed, and M'Candliss had to bitterly swallow the dust the hooves and wheels threw up as they left the encampment. He watched with frustrated eyes as the raiders wound up the trail to the narrow cleft and then passed from view.

Silence fell over the camp again. The night grew cooler, and the remainder of the *banditos* drew closer to their fires. After a time, most of them bedded down for the night.

A guard had been posted beside M'Candliss — a swarthy Mexican with a pitted face and a pot belly, who scowled fiercely whenever M'Candliss made a move. When the other outlaws turned in to their bedrolls, the guard threw a little more straw on the fire before him, sending the flames leaping once more; then he settled back and made himself comfortable.

M'Candliss searched the camp by the flickering firelight, trying to find some chance — any chance — for escape. The horses were nearby, including his claybank, but there was no way of reaching them. His guard didn't sleep, and the relaxed pose he showed was deceptive; the man was alert, and would come instantly alive at the slightest movement. Isabella still sat, head downcast, immovable as the mountains around her. And M'Candliss knew there was no possibility of help from any of the *banditos,* or from a rescue party, even if one could find this fortress.

He sat watching the guard, watching Isabella. The edginess inside him kept growing, and he knew it would prod him into action sooner or later. They were planning to kill him in Mexico City anyway; it was better if he died here, trying to escape so he could warn the delegates in Prescott.

After a string of minutes dragged away, Isabella finally stirred. M'Candliss watched her gather more meat and brown the chunks in animal fat. The fat sizzled and cracked in the pan, and the smoke was thick and fragrant; the smell made M'Candliss' empty belly cramp a little, even though he wasn't hungry. Then the woman stood, took a spoon, and walked with the still smoldering pan across the clearing toward M'Candliss and the guard.

The guard jumped to his feet as she neared. "What are you doing, woman?" he growled.

"I bring the *anglo* food," she said.

"No. Take it away." He waved his hand to emphasize the command.

"Miguel, don't be stupid," she snapped. "Do you want him to die from starvation? He has not had anything to eat all day. He must have food."

The two faced each other, both adamant.

"Do you wish to follow my father, Miguel?" Isabella demanded sharply. "Do you desire a bullet from Gueterma's *pistola* for having ruined his plans? The *anglo* is tied. He cannot escape. And I will feed him myself."

The guard looked indecisive; then, finally, he nodded. "As you will, then," he grumbled. "But do not be slow about it."

Isabella went to M'Candliss and knelt beside him, her body positioned so that her hands were hidden from the guard as he sat back down. She held up the spoon.

"Eat," she said. "It is badger meat, very good."

M'Candliss shook his head. "No," he said. But no sooner had he spoken the word than he felt something cold and hard along his wrist. He glanced down and saw that while Isabella was holding the spoon upraised in one hand, the pan balanced in her lap, her other hand was grasping a thin-edged knife. And she was slowly moving the blade along the rope that bound his hands.

"Eat," she urged, and M'Candliss managed to conceal his surprise and the fresh hope that surged inside him. He ate. The badger meat was hot and some of the grease burned his mouth, but he barely noticed. The motions of feeding and chewing hid the other actions, the cutting of his bonds. He moved his hands in rhythm to Isabella's sawing, until one by one the strands of rope parted.

"Pig!" Isabella said suddenly. "Dirty pig!"

The guard thought she was referring to M'Candliss and a harsh laugh came out of him. But M'Candliss saw the wetness of tears in her eyes, the trembling of her chin, and knew that she meant Gueterma and that her earlier avowals were false — a pretense so that later she could be free to help him. It had taken immense control and courage, more of both than most men he knew possessed.

"Isabella —"

"Do not talk. I do what must be done."

She changed positions, letting her skirt drape over his legs so that she could work on the bonds around his ankles, which had been retied by the guard. But her movements left her more vulnerable to the scrutiny of the guard. M'Candliss held his hands together, hoping that the dim light would not betray the strands of rope that hung from his wrists.

Isabella worked on the ankle ropes blindly, still feeding M'Candliss as she did so. But she hadn't managed to cut all the way through when M'Candliss' fears were realized.

"*Hai!*" the guard said and leaped up, frowning. "What are you doing?" He started to swing his rifle to bear.

Isabella whirled and threw the pan at him. It thunked off his shoulder, and the burning grease and hot bits of meat splashed and scalded his face; he threw up his hands, letting go of the rifle, and clawed at his eyes, screaming. "*Aieee!*"

M'Candliss rolled over, tried to stand. The rope

was still around his ankles, but when he kicked out the last strands parted. Lack of circulation made his legs feel prickly and cumbersome; he stamped down hard on them, willing them to respond.

"Hurry!" Isabella cried. "To the horses, before —"

But the screaming of the guard had already roused the camp. Isabella grabbed Miguel's rifle from where he had dropped it, then scrambled toward the horses. M'Candliss followed in an awkward, staggering run. The shouts of the *banditos* as they came out of their bedrolls, the screaming of the guard and the nervous whinnying of the horses created a confused din. Adding to it, a wild shot rang out.

Isabella cut the main picketing rope and threw herself bareback on a large bay. She fired the rifle — once, twice. Then, yelling at the top of her lungs, she kicked the horse into a hard run straight through the middle of the camp.

M'Candliss had swung onto his still-saddled claybank, and he raced after her. The rest of the horses bolted, snorting and whinnying, in all directions. M'Candliss knew that Isabella had begun yelling and had headed through the camp to give him time to escape in the darkness — an act of self-sacrifice that he wasn't about to accept. Riding after her, he sent a number of the *banditos* sprawling before they could recover and fire at her retreating back. The guard, Miguel, was still writhing on the ground, his cries the loudest of all.

Confusion reigned as the flying horses scattered the fires and the men.

Then they were out of the camp, heading for the pass, the claybank starting to close the distance between M'Candliss and the woman. He tried to keep himself between her and the bullets which now cracked forth from the regrouping outlaws. He hunched lower and urged the claybank to greater speed.

The trail grew steeper. Ahead was the opening in the cliff, a black mouth ready to swallow them. A shot plucked at M'Candliss' shirt; another left a furrow across his gunless holster. Then they were into the cleft, and the guns could no longer search them out. M'Candliss figured they had a short breathing space, perhaps as much as ten minutes' head start, depending on how fast the *banditos* could round up their horses and give chase. But ahead of them was the sentry, who might have been warned by the commotion.

"Isabella!" M'Candliss called. "Slow down!"

The woman reined up, allowing the claybank to close the last few feet between them. "What is it? Why do we stop?"

"The sentry," M'Candliss said. "We'll have to go around him."

"That is impossible. There is only one way out of the camp."

"How does the sentry get to his spot?"

Isabella thought for a moment, then replied, "There is a small trail just ahead. It leads to the little place where he sits."

"Show me," M'Candliss said, and she nodded. She gave him the pistol, a well-used, black-powder Harrington & Richardson. It was smaller than his own Colt .45, but the feel of it in his hand was just as reassuring.

Two minutes later Isabella showed M'Candliss where a narrow path led around a massive granite boulder and up the rock face. The horses picked their way carefully along it, while their riders peered into the gray shadows ahead. The trail was little more than a ledge cut into the wall; a false step by one of the horses would send them hurtling into the gorge below.

A hundred yards along, M'Candliss stopped and dismounted. "I'll go on alone from here, Isabella," he said.

"But —"

"You'll know soon enough whether it's me or him. While I'm gone, get the horses turned around; we'll be on our way that much faster. Or you will be if I don't make it."

He turned and continued up the boulder-strewn slope, pistol in hand. It seemed he was walking along the top of the world — in an eagle's nest with nothing but black sky stretching to infinity and sheer rock dropping hundreds of feet below. In the pale moonlight, he could make out the main trail winding up the slopes to the entrance to the camp; but the bottom of the gorge below was shrouded in Stygian blackness.

He moved cautiously, watching the trail's surface for loose stone. Once, a trickle of gravel dislodged by his boot showered over the edge, a miniature landslide that echoed in the stillness. The sentry would have heard that, he was sure — perhaps even have seen Isabella and him from his perfect lookout. He would be ready, waiting . . .

The attack came sooner than M'Candliss expected. Only a few more seconds had passed when the black figure suddenly sprang up in front of him, as if from nowhere. M'Candliss fired just as a belch of flame erupted from the shadowed form. Chips of rock stung his neck as the sentry's bullet whined off a boulder on M'Candliss' left; he heard a cry and a Mexican curse, then the clatter of the sentry's pistol on the rocky trail, and knew that his own shot had been truer and had winged the man.

But the bullet hadn't put the sentry down, or disabled him. He bellowed and charged. M'Candliss fired again, but missed in his haste and the darkness. He had no chance to fire a third time; the sentry was on him, grunting, thick-fingered hands groping for his throat. He lost his pistol as the man pinned him and tried to throw him sideways off the ledge. But M'Candliss was stronger; he got his own arms around the man's waist, squeezed, and managed to stand both of them straight up in a desperate embrace, so that neither was able to move the other for three or four seconds. Then, with a savage flexing of his muscles, he sent both of them stumbling into the rock wall, and the impact was enough to break the holds they had on each other. They broke apart like something splitting in half, and staggered in opposite directions on the trail.

When M'Candliss regained his balance he was ready to rush the sentry and end the fight then and there. But he hesitated when he saw the man reach to his belt and come up with something that glinted coldly in the moonlight — a long-bladed Mexican knife. M'Candliss looked for his dropped pistol, saw it near the edge of the precipice; but he knew he couldn't get to it before the sentry reached him with the knife. He set himself instead, crouching in a defensive stance as the *bandito* attacked with the knife held low.

M'Candliss feinted as the man lunged, and slapped the knife wrist aside; at the same time he caught hold of the other hand, thrust a leg across in front of the sentry, and broke the knife from the man's grip. In the struggle that followed, both men went down just inches from the drop-off.

The sentry tried to jam a forearm across M'Candliss' throat to crush his windpipe. M'Candliss kicked up with one leg and drove his boot into the sentry's ribcage. The man flew off him, but when he landed it was next to the fallen knife; he snatched it up. Before he could use it, M'Candliss scrambled to his feet and was ready when the man lunged again. This time the knife got inside M'Candliss' defensive tactics, and he felt the blade slash through his shirt, just nicking the skin of his sucked-in belly.

But the attack had thrown the sentry off balance, and M'Candliss kicked out again and felt

105

his boot sole jar against the man's hip. The sentry staggered backward, his wounded arm spraying droplets of blood as it windmilled over his head. He was right at the edge of the precipice, and he had no footing to regain his balance; he toppled backward and fell screaming out of M'Candliss' sight. There was a heavy thunking noise, cutting off the cry, and then fading echoes as the body tumbled into the gorge below.

M'Candliss leaned against the rock wall to catch his breath and wipe sweat from his face. Then he found Miguel's Harrington & Richardson, holstered, and made his way back to where he had left Isabella.

He didn't see her by the horses, and he realized she must have hidden herself in the rocks when she heard him approach; it was shadowed here and she wouldn't have been able to see who was coming down the trail. He called out to her, identifying himself. A moment later she appeared from behind an outcropping and hurried toward him. "You are all right, *Capitan* M'Candliss?"

In the moonlight, he was again struck by her resemblance to his murdered wife. He said tersely, "More or less. Let's get moving."

"Yes. The others — I think I have heard them coming."

M'Candliss swung into leather and eased his claybank forward, following the Mexican girl down the treacherous surface of the trail. Now he too could hear the pounding rhythm of hoofbeats in the distance, coming nearer from the valley below.

When they reached the main trail, the pale light of the desert moon illuminated the winding path along the rim of the great bowl. A dry night breeze murmured among the gigantic shadows of rocks outlined against the sky. Isabella led them through the narrow cleft between the towering cliff faces, and they dropped in a gradual descent along the trail. Some distance behind them, M'Candliss could hear the clatter of hooves against rock, the faint shouts of the raiders as they reached the top. He knew that he and Isabella were visible in the moonlight as they picked their way along, but the dips and curves were sufficient to prevent any accurate shooting from above.

They had descended to a point now where they could increase their speed. The trail had widened somewhat, become less precarious, and their horses' footing was surer. They made their way through the same shadowed canyons they had traversed on the trek to the *bandito* fortress, crossed the same mesquite-ridden arroyos and arid, rocky stream beds. And then, with the sounds of their pursuers faint in their ears, they were out of the Galiuros at last and into open land again.

M'Candliss motioned to the woman, pointing toward the southwest where the town of Adobe Junction lay, but she shook her head. "It is too far across the open desert," she said. "They are close enough already to use their rifles. We would stand little chance of reaching Adobe Junction."

M'Candliss knew she was right. "Is there another way around to the town? One that's not so open?"

"Yes," Isabella said. "To the south."

"That's private ranchland, isn't it?"

She nodded. "Mostly it is owned by a man named Gillette," she said with distaste.

Arlo Gillette, M'Candliss thought. The bigoted Mexican-hater and budding Territorial politico. He said, "How long will it take to go that way?"

"Several hours more. But it is our only hope, *verdad?*"

It looked that way to M'Candliss too. He didn't want to risk the extra loss of time, not when a whole trainload of American and Mexican lives depended on his swift action; nor did he much like the idea of trespassing on Gillette's rangeland, since there was no telling what kind of vigilante riders Gillette might have out protecting his claim. But the risk of crossing the open desert, of trying to outrun the pursuing *banditos,* was much greater. M'Candliss couldn't stop Gueterma from murdering all those men at Saddleback Gorge unless he himself remained alive in the interim.

"All right," he said grimly to Isabella. "South it is. Let's ride!"

He dug his bootheels into the claybank's flanks, Isabella bent low over the flowing mane of her bay, and they veered south through rumpled, craggy land toward the Gillette holdings.

NINE

They rode in silence for close to a half-hour, alternately running their horses at full speed and slowing them to a walk to conserve their energy. Isabella set a zigzagging course for them, skirting jagged outcroppings and the shadowed shapes of barrel cactus, twisted and tangled prickly pear, and giant saguaro like silent sentinels. From time to time, M'Candliss glanced over his shoulder. There was enough moonlight to let him see the plume of dust raised by the hooves of the raiders' horses. He judged that they were at least half a mile behind, and falling further back all the while.

As he rode, he calculated time and distance. If he and Isabella could skirt through Gillette's land without incident and reach Adobe Junction by late tomorrow night, there should be ample time to wire Lordsburg, New Mexico, the last station through which the delegates' train would pass before climbing into the Dos Cabezas Mountains and Saddleback Gorge, and have the stationmaster halt the train at that point. Then, with the safety of the dignitaries assured, M'Candliss could lead his company of Rangers, which should be waiting in Adobe Junction, to the mountain fortress, and put an end to Gueterma and his *banditos* once and for all.

More time passed. The claybank began to labor again, and M'Candliss could see that Isabella's bay was blowing heavily as well. When they topped a rise he signaled for the girl to slow her mount to a walk. Turning in his saddle, he looked behind them another time.

The dust cloud was a good three-quarters of a mile away now, he judged. He said as much to Isabella.

"Do you think they still pursue us?" she asked.

"Like as not," he said. "But then again, they might have turned tail and headed back into the mountains."

"Even if they still come, they will not catch us now."

"No," M'Candliss agreed, "they damned well won't. Isabella, do you know where Gueterma is holding Clement Holmes?"

"No. He did not tell any of us." Her mouth twisted bitterly. "He told us very little of his plans, yet we followed him like sheep. We were fools."

"Everybody's a fool at least once in his life," M'Candliss said. "Could he have had Holmes taken down into Mexico?"

"I think not, but I am not sure."

"Do you have any idea where he might be?"

She shook her head. "No, none."

Isabella fell silent after that. She stared out over

the barren land ahead, her face expressionless. M'Candliss had the feeling that she was thinking about her murdered father, the grim part she had had to play in order to help M'Candliss escape the fortress, the betrayal of her and her people by Gueterma. Inside, he felt a softness toward her. Now that her thinking had been cleared and rechanneled, she would make a good spokeswoman and champion of her people.

They walked their horses for a time, then put them back into a gallop. A trail appeared, angling westward, and Isabella led them onto it and over the brow of a ridge. Below were forty or fifty acres of sparse grazing land. Scattered along a hillside in the distance were a hundred or so head of cattle.

"Gillette's graze?" M'Candliss asked.

Isabella said that it wasn't. "It belongs to another," she told him, "a man called Miles. He, at least, does not have hatred in his heart for my people."

M'Candliss took another look at their back-trail. The dust cloud seemed to be dissipating, which meant either that the *banditos* had turned back or they had fanned out into smaller search parties that were staying off the trails. In either case, they no longer posed an immediate threat.

With Isabella leading the way, they rode down onto the graze. The claybank nickered softly, the way he always did when he smelled water. There had to be some close by, M'Candliss thought, to support the grass and the paloverde trees that grew here and there in the vicinity.

He and Isabella were a third of the way across the graze, angling west to skirt the hillside where the cattle were, when gunshots shattered the night's stillness.

They came from beyond the hillside — two, close together, followed by one from a different, larger weapon, then more of the first type. M'Candliss and the girl drew sharp rein. *Banditos?* he wondered. Doing battle with some of Miles' men, or one of the vigilante groups?

More shots cracked in rapid succession. Then the shooting stopped altogether and the night silence resettled. M'Candliss felt torn between going to investigate and giving the location of the shots a wide berth. He couldn't afford to get involved in anything that would put his life and his mission in jeopardy; and yet neither did he want to avoid trouble only to stumble into it blind somewhere else close by. If there were men in the area, he had to know who they were — local ranchers or more of Gueterma's raiders.

Two more shots erupted behind the hillside, and they made up his mind for him. He said to Isabella, "I'd better see what's going on. You wait here, over in that patch of rocks. If I'm not back in an hour, go on without me. Tell the people in Adobe Junction that Gueterma's behind the raiders and that he's planning to blow up the delegates' train at Saddleback Gorge."

She made a little gasping sound. *"Madre de*

Dios! That will cause war between your country and mine."

"Yeah. War is what Gueterma wants. He figures he can move right in and become *El Presidente.*"

"He told you this?"

M'Candliss nodded. "And your father over-heard; that's why he attacked Gueterma, and why Gueterma shot him."

"Mamapinga!" She said the Mexican obscenity with a mixture of savagery and awe. "We must stop him, *Capitan.* We must!"

"Don't worry," M'Candliss said grimly. "That's just what we're going to do." He left her and spurred his horse up the hillside. There was no more shooting, and he heard no other sounds as he rode. When he crested the hill he saw more grazing land and a small cattle pond some five hundred yards distant. In the moonlight he could make out two — no, three — men at the pond's near end.

The men wore wide Mexican sombreros and bandoliers of ammunition, and were on horse-back. They rode in the water, stirring it up so that it had a phosphorescent look in the moonshine. M'Candliss couldn't quite tell what they were doing, but it looked as though they were dragging something behind them by lengths of rope.

M'Candliss heeled the claybank along the brow of the hill, keeping to the cover of trees and rocks. A draw appeared then, cut downward along the edge of the slope, and when he turned into it the men dropped from sight. Near the bottom he found a path that led out of the draw onto the flat stretch of grazing land. Then he could see them again, moving slowly back and forth through the water as though planting seeds in earth. He was less than eighty yards from the pond, but he still could not make out what they were doing.

He started to edge closer, toward where a copse of trees grew on his left. But the claybank, with the scent of water strong in his nostrils, snorted and then nickered softly, and the sounds carried in the night's stillness. The three men reacted with swiftness and violence, dropping whatever they had been dragging through the water and drawing their weapons. Flame jumped from the hand of the rider on the right, and M'Candliss heard the bullet slash air over his shoulder. He ducked reflexively, hauled the Harrington & Richardson out of his holster, and kicked the claybank into a hard run straight at the three men.

Another shot sounded, this time from the man on the left, but it too missed wide. M'Candliss, riding low over the horse's neck, didn't fire until he was close enough to make his shots count; then he squeezed off twice, just as the one on the right cut loose at him again. M'Candliss' aim was better; that one jerked back, exposing his body, and M'Candliss shot into it. The man slumped forward, and his horse, whinnying with fright, bolted out of the pond. The one in the middle threw a quick, wild shot in M'Candliss direction, then raced after his wounded comrade. The third raider yelled as M'Candliss sent two more bullets

114

that way, slapped his mount, and galloped after the other two.

M'Candliss emptied his pistol at them, but in the moonlight he could see that none of the three dropped out of leather. Seconds later they were gone behind another low hill. The sound of their horses' hoofbeats faded to silence as M'Candliss slowed the claybank to walk.

When he neared the pond he saw movement in the grass to one side, the dark shape of a man on the ground. M'Candliss dismounted and went to the man in cautious strides. But the man was hurt, grunting with pain, and it was obvious that he was not one of the raiders; he wore cowboy clothes, and was a towheaded youth not long out of his teens. His shirt was bloody in the area of the right shoulder and there was a gash under his chin that was bleeding profusely.

"Thanks, Mister," the youth managed to say as M'Candliss knelt beside him. "I reckon you just saved my bacon. They'd have killed me sure if you hadn't come along."

"Mexican bandits?" M'Candliss asked.

"That's what I thought when they come swooping down on me. But I got a good look at one of them before they plugged me; hell, he was no more Mexican than I am."

"You ever see him before?"

"Matter of fact, yeah. One of Gillette's boys."

"Arlo Gillette?"

"That's him," the youth said. "Mr. Miles don't like Gillette worth a damn and neither do I. Troublemaker. And a damned fool too, if he's taken to hiring men who turn out to be bandits."

M'Candliss frowned as he tore the youth's shirt open. The chest wound, he saw, was not serious; a good deal of the blood came from the gash in the cowboy's jaw. "You'll be all right, son; you're not hurt bad. What's your name?"

"Ben Eckinshaw. You?"

M'Candliss told him. Then he asked, "What were you doing out here tonight?"

"Keeping an eye on things," Eckinshaw said. "Mr. Miles has been having trouble with them Mexican revolutionaries and he ordered a bunch of us out to patrol his range." He shook his head sheepishly, wincing. "Reckon I didn't do such a good job of patrolling, did I?"

"You did well enough. What were those three doing here?"

"Take a look at those sacks over to the pond," Eckinshaw said. "They'll tell you right enough."

M'Candliss straightened and went to the water's edge. In the shallow pond he saw the outline of three sacks, ropes attached with which the raiders had been dragging them. Wading in to the knees, he retrieved one and held it up. The water around it was a chalky white; the contents were half gone and dissolving rapidly, dropping more whiteness from the holes in the burlap. The sack had the head of a bull painted on one side, with words stenciled beneath it. The words read: *Stockyard Brand Pure Quicklime.*

"Careful there, Mr. M'Candliss," Eckinshaw

called. "You'll burn your hands if you ain't careful."

M'Candliss wasted no time. He dragged the sack from the pond, heeding the youth's advice to be careful, and hauled it up the bank far enough so that the runoff would not drain into the pond. Then he went in for the second and third bags and laid them alongside the first.

"You reckon enough of that lime got into the water to poison it?" Eckinshaw asked him when he was done.

"Might have. You'll have to run tests."

"Damn!"

"Tell me some things about Arlo Gillette," M'Candliss said. "Him and Mr. Miles been feuding long?"

"Wouldn't call it feuding, exactly. Mr. Miles don't like Gillette's way of doing business, nor all his hate talk about the Mexicans. He also don't like Gillette's plans for expansion."

"Expansion?"

"Gillette's been trying to get Mr. Miles to sell out to him. I reckon he's got visions of owning all the grazing land between the border and the Galiuros. Buildin' himself an empire, you might say. Some figure that's why he's trying to get into politics. Wants to own the whole goddamn Territory."

M'Candliss mulled this over, and the answers he came up with were hard ones. It could be that Gillette, in his greed, was taking advantage of the Mexican insurrection to do some private raiding of his own on neighboring ranches like Miles' — poisoning water, destroying property, shooting men, and making it all look like the work of Esteban's *revolucionarios*. Hell, it could even be that Gillette was mixed in with Gueterma, a pair of megalomaniacs banding together to create a reign of terror so that each could build his own private dictatorship on either side of the border. Gueterma had bought the services of Bruno Deney and Vern Beasley, among dozens, maybe even hundreds of others; why not the services of Arlo Gillette as well? And if Gillette *was* in cahoots with Gueterma, he might know where Clement Holmes was being held.

M'Candliss asked, "How far is Gillette's ranch from here?"

"About eight miles southwest, in Green Valley," Eckinshaw told him. "Why?"

"I'm thinking I might pay a call on him. Check on that hand of his who helped shoot you up."

"You want me to go along? I wouldn't mind facing that bastard myself."

"No," M'Candliss said. "You'd better get yourself doctored up. But I'd be obliged if you'd sell me your pistol. This one I've got is empty and I don't have fresh cartridges for it."

"Sell it to you, hell," Eckinshaw said. "You can have it. Least I can do in return for saving my life."

"Thanks. But you take this Harrington. Man's got to have a weapon these days, seems like, particularly in this neighborhood." He exchanged

118

pistols with the cowboy. "Your horse still around, or did they run him off?"

"Should be in those trees yonder," Eckinshaw said. "That's where I left him."

"I'll check. You figure you're steady enough to ride home?"

"Sure."

M'Candliss went into the trees, found Eckinshaw's horse, and led the animal back to the pond. Then he got directions to Green Valley, loaded the cowboy's old Colt, and shook hands with Eckinshaw. He mounted his claybank and rode out.

He debated going back to look for Isabella, to tell her if she was still there what he intended to do. But more than an hour had passed already, and two would have passed by the time he made it around to the other side of the hill. If she did as he'd told her — and he thought that she would — she'd be long gone by then. Let her go on alone; she was a strong woman, resourceful, and the sooner word of Gueterma's plans got back to Adobe Junction, the better. No use him wasting any more time, either. He'd see what he could find out at Gillette's ranch and then skedaddle for Adobe Junction himself.

Less than two hours later, M'Candliss walked his horse up a long rise flanked on either side by heavy thorn and brush. When he topped the rise he dismounted and dropped the reins. He stood motionless for several seconds, studying the valley floor below and what it contained.

Gillette's Bar-G ranch was at the near end — a large rambling house shaded by paloverde trees, a scatter of outbuildings, a corral and hay barn, a silo, and the big gallows-like windlasses of a pair of wells. All the outbuildings were dark including the bunkhouse. But lantern light showed behind some of the windows in the main house. The men who had poisoned the Miles pond and shot Eckinshaw were either in there, or they had already finished patching up the one who'd been wounded and had turned in at the bunkhouse.

On foot M'Candliss made his way down the brushy slope, careful not to break a branch or set a loose stone rolling. At the bottom were clumps of mesquite and a couple of paloverde, then a whitewashed fence and the ranchyard beyond. Standing in the shadows, he took a long look around at the buildings. Nothing stirred anywhere that he could see.

He moved ahead to the fence, climbed through, and then made his way across the yard, using the trees and one of the wells to cover his approach. When he reached the side wall of the ranch house he eased along to the nearest of the lighted windows and edged his head around to peer inside.

The room was opulent; luxury in a wilderness of cactus and sand. There were horsehair-stuffed chairs, each upholstered in a different color, and a heavy roll-top desk with silver handles and accessories. Hanging in the middle of the ceiling was a lighted candelabra with an old rose base and crystal drops, and long bands of twisted metal rather than the usual chains. The wallpaper, a rarity itself in this barren land, was bright with pink nosegays, and there were fine paintings on the wall of men on horseback, and hounds, and other mounted men in the process of jumping fences.

At first glance M'Candliss saw all of those and nothing more; the room seemed empty of habitation. But on a second, closer look, he realized that there was someone lying on a leather couch on the far side of the room. The couch was positioned so that its back was toward the window and it faced a cold fireplace; only the man's head was visible to M'Candliss, turned in profile. A silver-maned head, with just enough of the bearded features discernible for M'Candliss to recognize who it was.

Clement Holmes.

TEN

Holmes moved his head as M'Candliss watched, and a snuffling congested noise came from him, just audible through the window. At least he's alive, M'Candliss thought, tight-lipped. He tested the window sash, found that it was unlocked. He slid it up and stepped over the sill into the room.

He didn't move for a moment, listening. There were no sounds anywhere else in the house, no sounds at all except for Holmes' catarrhal wheezing. M'Candliss catfooted across to the couch. When he came around in front of it he saw that Holmes was trussed up with ropes, hand and foot, and that his aristocratic features were feverish and twisted into an expression of acute displeasure. His eyes were closed, but he seemed to sense M'Candliss' presence and opened them. They kept on opening, widening into a look of surprise and intense relief. He opened his mouth, but M'Candliss shook his head and put a finger to his lips. Holmes nodded and remained silent.

M'Candliss fished out his clasp knife, hunkered, and began to cut through the ropes that bound the diplomat. As he did so, he murmured,

"Are you all right, Mr. Holmes?"

"I am now. How did you know I was here?"

"I didn't," M'Candliss said. "Chalk it up to luck and Providence. Where's Gillette?"

"Somewhere in the house. At least he was a few minutes ago, the last time he looked in on me. How many men have you got with you, Captain?"

"None."

"None? Good God, Gillette has a dozen or more here at the ranch. How are we going to get away?"

"We'll manage. Nobody saw me come in, I'm sure of that. Do you think you can walk?"

"If I can't," Holmes said, "I'll hobble." He coughed, sniffled, and winced. "My grippe is much worse. I fear I have pneumonia."

"I hope not. But even at that, it'd be better than a bullet in your chest."

Holmes shuddered this time. "Yes. Neither Gillette nor that man at the mine, Deney, said so, but I gathered that would be my fate." He paused. "That was where I was taken after they kidnapped me in Adobe Junction — to an old silver mine nearby."

"I know," M'Candliss said. "We traced you there, but we showed up too late. They'd already moved you out."

"How did you trace me?"

"I'll explain everything later, sir."

M'Candliss finished sawing through the last of the ropes, put the knife away, and helped Holmes to his feet. The governor's man was a bit unsteady, but he was able to walk without aid. M'Candliss pointed him toward the open window across the room and followed a step behind him.

Footsteps sounded somewhere nearby, inside the house. M'Candliss stopped, his hand dropping to the butt of Eckinshaw's Colt. In the next second there was a noise beyond a pair of mahogany double doors. M'Candliss looked at the window, but they were too far away from it to make a run that way and hope to get through it in time. He shoved Holmes to one side, drew the Colt, and set himself just as one of the doors popped inward.

Arlo Gillette came into the study alone. He saw M'Candliss at the same time M'Candliss saw him, and his heavy face twisted with a mixture of disbelief and rage. He wore the same dark leather coat he had in Adobe Junction, still with its right side pulled back and tucked against the butt of his S&W .44. He snapped, "You!" viciously, and went for the pistol.

M'Candliss had no choice; it was kill or be killed. He fired just as Gillette cleared leather, and his bullet took the big man in the chest and spun him backward into the closed half of the doors. The rancher caromed off it and sprawled on his side in the open doorway, his hand still clutching the .44. One leg twitched, but it was nothing more than a spasm. Gillette was finished, and so were his grandiose plans to make Arizona Territory into his own private empire.

And so were M'Candliss and Holmes, if they didn't get out of there. The sound of the single shot had been loud in the room, and with the window open it would have been heard over at the bunkhouse. Holmes was already moving toward the window, a sickly expression on his face, but he was moving too slowly to suit M'Candliss. M'Candliss prodded him to the opening, pushed him through, and swung out himself. In the distance he could hear men shouting. He grabbed Holmes' arm and ran him away from the house, toward the cover of a paloverde nearby.

A man's voice yelled, "Hey, there! Hey, you, stop!"

Running, M'Candliss saw four dark figures rushing toward them across the yard, one of them carrying a lantern. Light from the lantern and from the moon outlined the pistols in their hands. M'Candliss snapped a shot at the men, and with his other hand he sent Holmes sprawling into the shadows of the paloverde just as two answering shots erupted.

Neither of the bullets came close. M'Candliss had already left his feet in a diving roll that carried him in next to Holmes in the pocket of darkness. He came up on his knees, looking back toward the men. They had scattered for cover, and the one with the lantern had blown out the flame. A bullet kicked up adobe a few feet to M'Candliss' left, and another splintered bark from the paloverde's trunk. The night had come alive with muzzle flashes and echoing gunfire.

The same voice as before shouted, "You get 'em, Pete?"

"Ain't sure," another voice answered. "Don't think I hit either one."

"Ben!" the first voice said. "Go inside the house and see if Mr. Gillette is all right."

"On my way."

M'Candliss knew he and Holmes were trapped behind the tree. There was open space on either side of them, and in the moonlight they would be clear targets if they moved out. If he'd been alone, he might have been able to make a run for the fence and the mesquite beyond. But with Holmes in his weakened condition, he'd never be able to get both of them to safety. He couldn't leave the diplomat . . . or could he?

An idea came to him. He tilted his head skyward. Clouds floated all around the moon, drifting pale wisps like thin strands of lace across its face; none of them concealed it long. But other clouds, bigger ones, were in the sky, and there was a chance that one of them would blot out the moonlight for a few seconds or more. It had to happen soon, though. Otherwise Gillette's men would surround them, and they wouldn't stand a chance then.

"What now, Captain?" Holmes asked. His voice was shaky, but he hadn't lost his nerve. After what he'd been through already, it would take more than what they were up against now to take away his courage.

"We've only got one chance," M'Candliss said.

"As soon as one of those clouds blocks off the moon, I'll make a run for the house."

"What for?"

"To draw their attention away from you," M'Candliss said, "and to give me room to maneuver. If I can create enough of a diversion, you might be able to make it clear."

"Are you sure that's the only way?"

"Dead sure. See that slope out beyond the fence? My horse is up at the crest. You get that far, ride out as fast as you can."

"Understood," Holmes said grimly.

"You know how to use a pistol?"

"Yes. I'm a good shot."

"Okay. Then you take this one." M'Candliss pushed Eckinshaw's Colt into the diplomat's hand.

"What about you? You'll be unarmed."

"Not for long, maybe. Gillette's gun is still in the study. If I can get inside there . . ."

He let the rest of it trail off. A heavy cloud formation was just starting to drift over the edge of the moon; and voices reached his ears again from across the ranch yard.

"He's dead, Clint!" It was the one who had gone to check on Gillette. "The boss is dead! Shot clean through the heart."

"Damn!" Clint said. He seemed to be the leader. "Pete, you get a look at the bastard over there with Holmes?"

"Yeah. It's that Ranger, M'Candliss."

Pause. "Well, he won't get away this time. He's

127

a dead man for sure — him and Holmes both."

There was more talk, but the men lowered their voices and M'Candliss couldn't hear what they were saying. Not that he needed to hear; he knew they were working out the best way to deploy so they could surround the paloverde. The time to move was now, moonlight or no moonlight.

Tensing, he glanced skyward again. The cloud formation had swallowed more of the moon, and the pale light in the ranch yard was fading. He whispered to Holmes, "It's now or never. Don't do any shooting unless you have to, and don't make any noise. Make them think you're wounded or already dead."

"Just as you say."

Three-quarters of the moon was obscured when M'Candliss made his run for the ranch house. The element of surprise was on his side; he had covered a third of the distance, running in a weaving crouch, before they spotted him and sent the first shot his way. He felt a bullet tug at his pantleg and sting across the back of his calf, and he left his feet again in another diving roll. A volley of slugs slashed the air above him as he rolled into the shadows along the side wall, unhurt.

He jumped up and raced to the open study window. Swung himself over the sill and landed running on the hardwood floor within. The body of Arlo Gillette was still sprawled in the open doorway, the S&W .44 clenched in his stiffening fingers; M'Candliss bent and pried the weapon free. Then he stepped over the dead man, went down a hallway toward the back of the house, and finally emerged in the kitchen.

He stopped there when he saw the cookstove in one corner. A fire had been built inside, and the metal glowed a dull rust-red. Quickly, M'Candliss bent and pulled open the door at the stove's bottom, revealing the hot coals inside. He picked up a small scoop shovel which lay nearby and dipped out several of the coals; then he straightened again and turned toward the archway. Beyond it lay a parlor which faced into an open-air central patio.

Floor-length velvet drapes covered one wall of the parlor, and M'Candliss carried the shovelful of coals there, dropped the red-hot embers on the material. Flames shot up almost immediately, consuming the drapes and sending tongues upward toward the beamed ceiling. It would not take long, he knew, before the whole room was ablaze.

He darted through another archway into the center patio. On his left was one of the wooden support pillars for the low portico which covered the section just beyond the arch. Moving there, he climbed the pillar and swung himself up onto the portico by way of its upturned lip. He eased along the gradual slant until he stood at the wall of the house's second story. By stretching full-length he could grasp enough of the tile roof to pull himself up.

He climbed the tiles carefully, boot soles seeking out and gripping weather-eroded chinks.

When he gained the roof's peak he crouched there, looking into the darkened yard. Some of Gillette's men were shouting, running toward the house. He couldn't see into the heavy shadows behind the paloverde where he'd left Clement Holmes; Holmes was either still there or he had made it to cover somewhere beyond the fence, because there was no sign of him anywhere else.

The fire was spreading rapidly through the interior of the house; flickering light that cast grotesque shadows on the ground below told M'Candliss that. He moved sideways along the roof's peak, toward the rear. When he got there he looked down on a low porch roof similar to the portico in the central patio. He lowered himself onto the porch roof, crawled along it to where he could see into the yard directly below.

One of the hands was there, pistol drawn, staring at the rear door as if waiting for someone to come bursting out. M'Candliss crept forward until the toes of his boots touched the edge, crouching with his left arm out for balance. Then he jumped out and down.

He landed just to the man's right. The hand gave a startled gasp, whirling, but he had no time to cry out a warning or to bring his pistol to bear. M'Candliss clubbed him alongside the head with the barrel of Gillette's .44. The man let out a low, muffled sigh and dropped to the ground at M'Candliss' feet.

M'Candliss took a quick look around him. There was no one else nearby, although he could hear the sounds of men shouting from the front section of the house. He could also hear the rumbling crackle of the fire as it raced from surface to surface inside the adobe walls.

He ran straight ahead, toward the looming shape of the stable. He would have preferred to go the other way, around to where the paloverde was, to see if Holmes was still there and to help him get away if he was. But that would have been suicidal; he'd have had to cross too much open ground, and Gillette's men were swarming around the house. All he could do was to get himself clear of the area and hope that Holmes had done the same.

Reaching the stable, M'Candliss moved around behind it and circled the split-rail fence until he was almost parallel with the burning ranch house. None of the hands were here; they were all at the far side of the yard. He slipped between the rails into the corral. A half-dozen horses moved on the hard-packed adobe, turned skittish by the commotion and the fire. He managed to calm one of the animals, to slip a halter over its head that he found hanging carelessly from one of the fence posts. Then he led it to the corral gate and out to the side of the stable.

The stable's bulk hid both him and the horse as he took it around the rear of the bunkhouse. Half a minute later, he found a side gate in the fence enclosing the ranch yard. He opened it, swung onto the horse's bare back, and rode through into the darkness beyond.

It took him ten minutes to circle through the mesquite, along the near ridge of the valley, to the top of the brushy slope where he'd left his claybank. When he found the horse he didn't see any sign of Holmes, not there nor on the slope below, and he thought he was going to have to risk going down to the ranchyard again. But then, as he dismounted, a figure appeared from behind one of the larger bushes and called out to him softly.

"Captain! It's Clement Holmes."

There was relief in the voice, and relief in M'Candliss too as he moved over to join the diplomat. "You all right, sir?" he asked.

"Yes. Scared to death, but not harmed. I slipped away not long after you disappeared inside the house."

"You should have ridden out as soon as you got up here," M'Candliss said.

"I know. And I was about to when I heard you coming just now. But I was worried about you, Captain. I thought there might be something I could do to help you. I owe you my life, after all."

"We're both safe, that's the main thing," M'Candliss said. "And we've got a lot of other lives to worry about."

Below, in the ranch yard, Gillette's house was a blazing pyre. In the reddish glow of the flames, M'Candliss could see some of the men milling about in a confused way, while others had formed a bucket brigade at one of the wells. It wouldn't be long before they realized both M'Candliss and

Holmes had escaped, and when they reorganized they would likely send out a search party. Both he and the governor's man would have to be well on their way by then if they hoped to reach Adobe Junction without trading any more lead.

He took Holmes' arm, steered him to the claybank. When the diplomat had mounted, M'Candliss swung onto the horse he had liberated from the corral and led the way back toward a road he had seen earlier. The road pointed southwest, the direction of Adobe Junction, and he thought that it would lead straight to the town across the desert's rim.

When they reached the trail they rode hard and in silence for the better part of an hour. Clement Holmes was a good horseman; despite his weakened condition, there was no problem along those lines. Nor was there any problem with pursuit. After a time M'Candliss could see a dust cloud in the far distance behind them, but there was little chance that Gillette's men could overtake them or that they would keep up the chase as far as Adobe Junction. M'Candliss knew men like that, and with their boss dead, the odds were they would disband and light a shuck for other parts before morning.

The first time M'Candliss slowed the pace, to give their horses a breather, he told Holmes everything that had happened in the past few days. The governor's man expressed shock at the news about Gueterma's duplicity, and outright horror at the plan to blow up the delegates' train at Saddleback Gorge.

"My God, Captain," Holmes said, "we can't let that happen. We can't! It would mean certain war between our country and Mexico."

"It won't happen," M'Candliss told him. "Isabella Ortiz will get to Adobe Junction before we do, and she'll spread the word to my men. Flynn and Meckleburg will send a wire to Lordsburg in plenty of time to stop the train when it reaches that point."

"I hope you're right, Captain," Holmes said grimly.

"Don't worry, sir. I am."

But he wasn't. For one of the few times in his career, M'Candliss, as he would discover before the end of another day, was dead wrong.

ELEVEN

It was late afternoon, coming on five o'clock by M'Candliss' stemwinder, when they reached Adobe Junction.

The day had been very hot, with the sun a huge fiery disc that spread shimmers of heat and baked their skin as they rode. They had had no apparent pursuit since daybreak, and encountered no one on the road except a bearded man driving a traveling fix-it wagon. Several times they had stopped to rest, once at a waterhole near the road to ease the painful dryness in their throats and to freshen their mounts. Holmes grew weaker as the day progressed, but he made no complaint. He was determined to reach the town under his own power; there would be time enough then, he told M'Candliss, to doctor his grippe and to worry about the threat of pneumonia.

The flagging strength of both Holmes and the horses forced them to slow down considerably, and when the wooden buildings of Adobe Junction finally came into view through the heat haze, they were moving at little more than a walk. Holmes managed a weak smile and sat up straighter in the claybank's saddle.

"We made it, Captain," he said.

"Didn't you reckon we would?"

"There were times when I had my doubts. About myself, that is — never about you. You're a damned strong man, M'Candliss. Damned strong."

"So are you, sir. And that's a fact."

They rode across the last mile of mesquite and cactus and ironwood in silence. When they passed through the small Mexican quarter and turned onto the dusty main street, M'Candliss saw a crowd of townspeople in front of the adobe building that housed Sheriff Tucker's office and the jail. He leaned forward over his horse's neck and peered at the crowd. He could make out Sheriff Tucker's houndlike face, but he saw no sign of Isabella Ortiz. Nor did he see Flynn or Meckleburg or any of the rest of his company of Rangers.

A man at the edge of the gathering saw them coming and let out a shout. The crowd surged around them, buzzing excitedly as they drew rein and M'Candliss dismounted. He helped Holmes out of his saddle, then turned to face the sheriff.

"Hell, M'Candliss," Tucker said, "you're a sight for sore eyes. You too, Mr. Holmes."

"That goes double for us," M'Candliss told him. "Did Isabella Ortiz ride in today?"

"Sure did. More'n two hours ago. She's resting over to the hotel."

M'Candliss was relieved that she was safe. He

136

nodded. "Then you know about Gueterma and what he's planning to do at Saddleback Gorge."

Anger tightened Tucker's mouth. And something else that might have been grim frustration. "Yeah," he said, "she told us. But —"

"Did you send a wire to Lordsburg to stop the delegates' train?"

"No, goddamn it. We couldn't."

"Why the hell not?"

The telegraph operator, Cable, who had been standing nearby, stepped forward. "Lines are down," he said. "Been down since early morning. Not a thing we can do about it, feller."

M'Candliss cursed. He knew what had happened — the *banditos* who had chased Isabella and him from the mountain fortress had realized that he would try to warn the delegates' train by wire if he reached Adobe Junction. When they hadn't been able to catch him, they had cut the telegraph lines.

"We been tryin' to decide what to do," Tucker said. "Nearest town with a telegraph office is San Ameron, but it's half a day's ride. No way to get there and send a wire in time, even if their lines are still up."

Clement Holmes ran a hand across his gritty face. He looked exhausted, but his eyes blazed under their sunburnt lids. "How far is Saddleback Gorge from here?" he asked the sheriff.

"Too far to get there before the train does."

"Are you certain of that?"

"He's right, sir," M'Candliss said. He had done

137

some fast computing, remembering Governor Shannon's wire of two nights ago. It had said that the delegates' train would arrive in Prescott at noon tomorrow. Figuring some three hours between the Territorial capital and Saddleback Gorge, that meant the train would pass over the trestle at roughly nine a.m. It was now almost six — and it would take a full day, even pushing their horses to maximum speed all the way, to reach Saddleback Gorge. "There's just no way it can be done."

"You and your men have got to try, Captain," Holmes said, "no matter how futile it seems. We can't give up — not with so many lives at stake."

"We're not going to give up," M'Candliss said tightly. He looked at Sheriff Tucker. "Where are all my Rangers, Sheriff? There was supposed to be a company sent here from the nearest garrison —"

"So there was," Tucker told him. "But they all took out this mornin' to scout around for you, long before that Mexican gal showed up."

"Flynn and Meckleburg too?"

"Flynn went with 'em. Lieutenant Gordon left Meckleburg behind to keep an eye on things. He's over at the hotel, lookin' after Miz Ortiz."

"Do you know where the Rangers went?"

"They didn't tell me," Tucker said. "But I reckon up into the Galiuros, lookin' for some sign."

M'Candliss cursed again, It was unlikely that Gordon and the rest of the Rangers would find the *bandito* fortress. And there was no telling when they would return — possibly not until some time tomorrow, when it would be much too late.

Fifteen hours — that was all the time they had. But what could they do, even if his men were here? There was just no chance to reaching Saddleback Gorge by horseback in that amount of time . . .

An idea struck him. He asked Tucker, "Is there a locomotive down in the rail yard? A switch engine, if nothing else?"

Tucker scowled. "Reckon there is, sure. What you got in mind?"

"We can't stop the delegates' train in Lordsburg," M'Candliss said, "but we might be able to get to Saddleback Gorge and spring Gueterma's trap before the delegates get there. A locomotive and a couple of cars just might make it from here to the gorge before nine tomorrow morning."

There were excited murmurs from the crowd, and the sheriff nodded emphatically. "By gum, it might work at that!"

"We can't wait around," M'Candliss said. "We'll have to get under way as soon as possible — within the half hour."

"We can do that, all right," Tucker promised. "Maybe we won't have your Rangers, but we'll have plenty of men and guns to side our run." He turned toward the assembled townspeople. "Isn't that right, men?"

The reaction of the able-bodied citizens and

cowboys in the crowd was immediate and vociferous. They had wanted a chance to strike back at the murdering *banditos* who had spread so much terror across their land, and now that chance had come. They swarmed around Tucker and M'Candliss, volunteering their services as many of them had before, after the *bandito* raid at *El Sacacorchos.*

Taking charge, the sheriff told them they were all deputized. "Grab your rifles and some extra ammunition," he ordered them, "and meet us at the rail yard, quick as you can. Now move out. Get cracking!"

The men hurriedly scattered in all directions.

Clement Holmes said to Tucker, "I'm going along too, Sheriff. You'll have to supply me with a rifle —"

"You're not going anywhere, sir," M'Candliss told him, "except straight to bed."

"Damn it, Captain, I want to be in at the finish of this business —"

"I know you do. But you're in no condition to make a trip like we're planning. You need rest and doctoring, or you'll wind up sure with pneumonia."

Holmes started to argue further, but a spasm of coughing overcame him. By the time he had gotten it under control, M'Candliss had taken hold of his arm and was steering him up the street toward *La Hacienda.* The governor's man glanced at M'Candliss, wiping his eyes with the back of one hand, but he made no protest. He seemed to

140

have accepted the fact, however reluctantly, that he was too weak for any more activity.

They were halfway to the hotel when its front door burst open and Meckleburg came charging out onto the boardwalk. As soon as he saw M'Candliss and Holmes, he veered toward them.

"Cap, Mr. Holmes — am I glad to see you! I couldn't hardly believe it when I heard all the commotion and looked out the window and there you were at the jail. I'd about given you both up for dead."

"Providence has been on our side," M'Candliss said. "So far. Let's hope it stays that way."

"What happened? Where'd you find Mr. Holmes?"

"I'll fill you in on that later."

Meckleburg looked along the much less populated street. "Where'd everybody scatter to?"

M'Candliss told him about the planned race by rail for Saddleback Gorge.

"Hell," Meckleburg said, "why didn't I think of that? It's a good idea, Cap."

"Good or bad — it's the only idea we've got."

With Meckleburg helping, M'Candliss took Clement Holmes inside the hotel and got him settled into bed in the room from which he'd been abducted. Exhaustedly, the diplomat shook M'Candliss' hand.

"Good luck, Captain," he said.

"Thank you, sir. We'll need it."

In the hallway outside, M'Candliss found Isabella Ortiz waiting when he and Meckleburg left the governor's man. She had been resting in one of the rooms just down the hall and she had heard them come in. She looked tired, but her eyes were bright and eager. She seemed more than a little glad to see him alive and well.

M'Candliss quickly explained what he and the townspeople were going to do. Isabella wanted to go along too, but he vetoed the idea. "Somebody has to stay here and keep an eye on Mr. Holmes," he said.

"Gueterma murdered my father," she said. "Would you deny me the opportunity to kill him, *Capitan*? Or at least to watch him die?"

"I would and I am," M'Candliss answered. "Your people need you, Isabella, just as our people need Clement Holmes. You can't afford to risk your life any more right now."

Isabella tried to argue, but M'Candliss remained adamant. He had developed a fondness for the Mexican woman — a deeper fondness that he was willing to admit to himself at the moment — and he was determined to keep her out of harm's way. There was no telling what sort of carnage might take place at Saddleback Gorge; it was a certainty that there would be shooting, in any event, and that there would be casualties. Isabella wasn't going to be one of them.

He finally convinced her to stay put and keep watch on Holmes. Then he and Meckleburg got their rifles and hurried downstairs. At the desk, M'Candliss told the fat, bespectacled clerk to fetch the druggist who had tended Vern Beasley.

Holmes was going to need both the druggist's medical knowledge and his supply of bottled medicine in order to regain his health.

When the two Rangers arrived at the rail yard they found Sheriff Tucker deep in conversation with an elderly, round-featured man whose name turned out to be Frederickson. He was a retired engineer and keeper of the Adobe Junction roundhouse, and Tucker had conscripted him. From the looks of Frederickson's eager face, he hadn't had to twist the man's arm to get him to agree to the task.

Several other men were already in the yard, some of them talking in small groups, others coupling a single passenger car to an old, big-wheeled, big-boilered 4-4-0 locomotive. The boiler had been fired, and steam chuffed out of the engine's straight stack. Her rhythm sounded unsteady to M'Candliss, but Frederickson assured him that she was sturdy and dependable. She had counterbalanced wheels, he said, to minimize "hammer-blow" on the tracks, and big sandboxes to provide assistance to track friction. She'd get them to Saddleback Gorge in thirteen hours or less if any locomotive could; Frederickson guaranteed it.

M'Candliss took that guarantee with the grain of salt it merited, but he said nothing. He merely nodded and turned to help Tucker round up the assembled men and herd them into the passenger car. The last of the deputies arrived while they were doing that; when they had taken their places inside, M'Candliss counted a total of twenty-three men — hardly an army, but enough to hold their own against Gueterma and his band of renegades. He left Meckleburg and Tucker to handle things in the car and climbed up into the cab with Frederickson and a fireman.

Minutes later, shortly before seven o'clock, the locomotive's rods began to grind and they surged out of the yard under a full head of steam.

TWELVE

Sunset flamed in the west; the Galiuro peaks cast blue dusk shadows, and the tracks gleamed golden before the onrushing locomotive. Inside the cab, M'Candliss squinted as the sun fired the glass windscreen set on an angle outside the open side window. There was sweat on his bare back, mixed with soot; he had shed his shirt and was helping the fireman, a man whose name he never learned, shovel crumbly coal into the firebox. The heat in the cab was intense, much hotter than the desert sun had been during the long day's ride.

After they had crossed an expanse of desert northeast of Adobe Junction, the terrain had begun to roughen with jagged rock formations and the right-of-way had become narrower and more winding. Now thick brush on steep slopes hemmed in the speeding one-car train.

Frederickson, at the throttle, puffed furiously on a stubby pipe and alternated between putting his head out through the window to check the tracks ahead and watching the steam pressure gauge. The fireman had his eye on the gauge too, and he seemed much less confident than Frederickson was.

"I hope to Christ she don't blow," he said to M'Candliss. "This hog was retired years ago. Hell, she's got more patches on her than I've got on my Levi's."

Frederickson overheard that. "Bullshit," he said. He tapped the pressure gauge; the black needle shimmied. "She can take plenty more than we're giving her. Don't worry."

"So you say," the fireman grumbled. He tossed another shovelful into the firebox. "Damn coal is lousy too."

Frederickson scowled and pulled the whistle cord; a sharp blast echoed from the long tube atop the boiler hump. He tugged the cord again, and then a third time. M'Candliss thought that it was because he was remembering the highballing days of his youth and liked to hear the sound of the whistle. There was nothing on or around the tracks to get in their way.

The locomotive sped on. Night shadows began to lengthen as they climbed higher and the westering sun dipped behind bluffs and ridges. The sunset colors faded out of the sky and the deep purple of twilight seeped in in their place. It would be dark in another few minutes.

M'Candliss laid his shovel down and stood at the side bulkhead to take some of the hot cindered breeze. As he did so, he considered the geography. The Galiuros extended from below the Mexican border up in a north-northwesterly line into the middle of Arizona Territory; the Dos Cabezas were to the northeast of them. Two major rail lines crossed into the southern half of Arizona from New Mexico and the State of Texas; the main line branched at Lordsburg in New Mexico, one going to Phoenix and the other to Tuscon. There was a connecting line between Tucson and the Phoenix branch, and this was the spur on which they were traveling. It linked in just east of Spanner, on the San Pedro River, and some miles beyond the switch were the Dos Cabezas and Saddleback Gorge.

The *bandito* fortress was located in the southern section of the Galiuros; Gueterma and his raiders would have traveled almost due north from there. This train was faster than their wagons and horses, but the raiders had had a day's head start and a more or less direct path. M'Candliss put his head out of the side window and counted the telegraph poles strung along this section of right-of-way, checking his stemwinder as he did so. It was a little over two minutes each between the poles, which meant that the train was making just over thirty miles an hour.

Not fast enough, M'Candliss thought. Unless they could pick up more speed, particularly on the downgrades, it seemed likely that Gueterma's raiders would reach Saddleback Gorge and have time to deploy before M'Candliss and the posse arrived.

The engineer, Frederickson, hooked the reverse bar up another notch and widened the throttle

147

full open. The whir of the drivers, the beat of the trucks, the bark of the exhaust created a thunderous sound in M'Candliss' ears. The air was clogged with cinders and smoke as the locomotive, her side rods flashing, her wheel flanges screaming on the curves, roared on through the gathering darkness.

M'Candliss picked up his shovel and went to the tender for more coal. Night closed around them; Frederickson switched on the locomotive's headlamp. The air outside cooled, and that lessened the heat somewhat in the cab. But M'Candliss kept right on sweating, and his muscles ached with strain and fatigue. He had been two days without sleep; he knew he was going to have to quit soon and get some rest. Otherwise, neither his mind nor his reflexes would be functioning worth a damn when the train reached Saddleback Gorge.

The tracks began to wind across a long, narrow Galiuro valley, between high ridges furred with trees. The headlamp made shiny ribbons of the rails ahead, cast light into the brush-laden gullies and stretches of sloping rock walls that flanked the right-of-way. M'Candliss' stemwinder said the time was getting on toward ten o'clock.

His mind felt sluggish, his arms as if lead weights were tied to them. He said finally to the fireman, "Can you handle the box alone? I'm about all in."

"Hell, yes, he can handle it," Frederickson said before the fireman could answer for himself. "Get

148

yourself some rest, Captain."

The fireman nodded agreement. "Go ahead. No problem."

"Thanks," M'Candliss said. "I'll be back before dawn. I want to be here in the cab when we reach the gorge."

M'Candliss laid his shovel down again, scrambled across the coal in the tender, and let himself down on the small platform behind it. There was little room and the train rolled and pitched at the speed it was traveling. The passenger car ground against the pin-coupler and swayed erratically in a backlashing motion. M'Candliss held onto the brake wheel on the tender and judged the leap.

He sprang as the car and the locomotive tilted the same way. His boots hit the plank duck-board walkway, and his hand tightened around an iron rung of the ladder leading to the roof. He firmed his hold, then opened the door and stepped inside the car.

The interior was warm with humanity, yet very quiet. The wall lamps had been lit, and the pitching motion cast dancing patterns of light and shadow over the faces of the score of men sitting or standing. Their features were all hard-set, fired with determination.

M'Candliss felt a sense of satisfaction as he looked them over. They weren't his highly trained Rangers, and they had no real experience at the kind of battle they were rushing toward; they were just plain everyday folk, the average citizens of his Territory, men who had gladly broken out of the mold of routine living to defend their homes in this crisis. And that made them plenty good enough when push came to shove. These were the men who had built Arizona into a unified territory and who would one day make it a state — men who didn't need the notoriety of outlawry to make them part of history, who in just living had greater courage and faced more danger and hardship than the killers and thieves whom M'Candliss fought.

Alfredo Ortiz had been wrong, very wrong, when he said that the *anglos* had become soft. The men in this car, M'Candliss thought, were hardier and more resilient and unflinching than any other set of men in the history of the nation. He would have been proud to have any one of them in his band of Rangers, and to call any one of them his friend.

He squeezed through the packed car to where Meckleburg and Sheriff Tucker were sitting on a bench next to a cold pot-bellied stove. "Everything all right in the cab, Cap?" Meckleburg asked, making room for him.

"So far. We're running wide open."

"Figured we were."

Tucker extracted a large silver Elgin International from his vest pocket as M'Candliss sat down. "After ten," he said. "Reckon we still got twelve hours or so left to go."

M'Candliss nodded. "I figure we'll get to Saddleback Gorge some time between eight and nine."

"Should be plenty enough light by then for accurate shootin'," Tucker observed.

"If we're lucky, Gueterma and his bunch won't be there yet. Then we'll be able to stop the delegates' train on the other side of the trestle."

The sheriff jerked his chin toward the other men. "They'd be disappointed, if it came to that," he said. "They're spoilin' to settle a few accounts."

"They'll get their chance, like as not," M'Candliss said. "Sooner or later."

Meckleburg was studying him in the unsteady lamplight. "You look plumb tuckered, Cap. Maybe you'd best get yourself some sleep."

"Yeah. Might be a good idea if everyone else did the same. The more alert everybody is come morning, the better our chances."

"You're right about that," Tucker agreed. He stood up and called for attention, and when he had it he passed along what M'Candliss had said.

There were murmurs from the men, and one complained, "How the hell can a body sleep in a damned old rattler like this?" But they settled down on the wooden seats and benches, while Tucker went around extinguishing all of the lamps. Within minutes the steady roar of steel on steel was punctuated by thickened breathing and an occasional snore.

It took M'Candliss longer than the rest to get to sleep, despite his fatigue. Thoughts kept tumbling through his mind — of the delegates in the Prescott train, of Gueterma and his *banditos,* of what awaited him and the posse at Saddleback Gorge. And, strangely, of Isabella Ortiz. It had been a long while since a woman had gotten under his skin — not since the death of his wife. But there was no denying that Isabella had. Nothing could ever come of it, of course; she was pledged to help her people in their struggle for freedom and a better life, and he was pledged to help Governor Shannon build Arizona into the great state it would someday be. Yet that didn't stop a man from dreaming . . .

M'Candliss slept fitfully, but when a whistle blast from the cab woke him just before dawn, he felt rested and alert. His joints were stiff from the cramped position he had been in; he walked around some to work out the stiffness. Some of the other men were awake as well, including Tucker and Meckleburg.

"I'm hungry enough to eat a horse," Meckleburg said, "saddle and all. We should've thought to bring some grub, Cap."

"You'll fight better on an empty stomach," M'Candliss told him. "And you'll appreciate your next meal even more."

M'Candliss returned to the locomotive just as Frederickson cut loose with three short blasts and one long one on the whistle. They were approaching the junction of the main line between Lordsburg and Phoenix, the old engineer explained. The whistle blasts were to let the signalman at the switching point know they were coming and to split the switch.

"Don't have to stop, that way," Frederickson said. "We'll cannonball straight on through."

"What if there's another train coming from Lordsburg?" M'Candliss asked.

"Next one scheduled through is at four this afternoon. If we get flagged onto a siding, it'll be because of the delegates' special coming through early; then we'd know they got over the trestle safe and sound."

The switch was split when they reached the junction. Frederickson waved at the signalman as the one-car train rocketed onto the main line, heading east. They passed the siding used to shunt one train onto so another could pass by. The delegates' train hadn't cleared the trestle yet; the race against time was still on.

M'Candliss relieved the tired and soot-blackened fireman as dawn broke. They were into the Dos Cabezas now, climbing; a deep coppery color spread through the sky. M'Candliss could hear the valves popping and cracking, and the old cylinders and drivers were laboring on the grade. He watched Frederickson shut down the steam a little to relieve some of the boiler pressure, heard the popping diminish almost instantly.

A few miles later they reached the top of the grade and started along the rim of a canyon. On their left, the slope was steep and heavily bouldered. On their right, the canyon face was less steep, more like a tilted slope than a wall.

"Coming on the gorge," Frederickson yelled

over the engine noise. "Won't be long now — another few minutes."

M'Candliss checked his stemwinder. The time was seven-forty. Laying his shovel down, he stood tensed and waiting for the long, spidery trestle bridging the canyon to come into view.

Ahead the tracks made a long curve. Frederickson kicked the brakes on lightly as they started into it, kicked them off again. All around them was desolate beauty, a soaring chain of giant peaks and naked rock that glistened against the deepening blue of the morning sky.

The slopes steepened on both sides as the train cut the segments. Then, swiftly, the terrain leveled out into a small plateau — a ledge that projected over the now dizzying depths of the canyon.

Saddleback Gorge.

Directly ahead the trestle loomed, a spindly cross-hatch of wooden beams that looked like a thin spiderweb linking the two sides of the chasm. The trestle curved slightly to give its length more rigidity against the heavy winter winds and snows. It looked far more fragile than it was.

"Over a hundred yards long," Frederickson said. "First three they tried to build didn't last a season —"

Whatever else the engineer was going to say was lost. He cried out suddenly, wheeled and fell away from the throttle; M'Candliss caught him, saw blood appear on his shoulder, and at the same time heard the faint echoing crack of a rifle above the pounding of the trucks. Then there were more cracks; bullets slapped against the engine and tender, pinging off the iron, thudding into wooden surfaces.

"Down!" M'Candliss yelled to the fireman. The other man threw his shovel aside and hit the deck of the cab. M'Candliss crouched over the fallen Frederickson, pistol out and gripped tight in his hand. They had won the race against time in the sense that they had reached Saddleback Gorge ahead of the delegates' train; but they had lost what might be the most important part of the race, just as he had been afraid they would.

Gueterma and his *banditos* had already arrived and were hidden in the rocks above, raining lead down on the speeding train.

THIRTEEN

M'Candliss made an instant decision, based on instinct and on what he had seen at the *banditos'* mountain fortress. He levered up and leaped to the controls; the train was almost to the trestle now, and there wasn't a moment to spare.

He slammed the throttle shut, twisted the brake handle, and wiped the gauges clean. The brake shoes ground against the wheels, making the locomotive, tender, and passenger car buck and reel crazily. The drivers screamed and locked tight, sliding along the rails.

Frederickson had managed to raise up on one hip; the wound in his shoulder wasn't crippling. "What the blazes are you doing?" he yelled at M'Candliss.

"Stopping this hog!"

"Hell's fire — *why?*" the fireman snapped. He clambered to his feet and started for M'Candliss. "Are you crazy? They're shooting at us out there! Once we get across the trestle we'll be safe!"

"The hell we will! There's dynamite on that trestle! They won't let us get across; they'll blow us up!"

He flung the reverse bar over and opened the throttle. The fireman's horrified cry of "My God!" was lost in the sudden thunder of the drivers locking, spinning backward. Outside, the raiders' bullets whizzed all around the train; the men in the passenger car were returning fire now, unaware of the sure death that lay ahead of them if M'Candliss failed to stop the locomotive in time.

The laboring engine was within a few yards of the trestle before the brake shoes locked fully. The scream of metal on metal lessened; the old 4-4-0 shimmied, seemed to want to stand on its nose. They ground to a shuddering halt. Steam hissed mightily from the ancient boiler, and patched steel groaned in protest against the strain.

M'Candliss left the controls and dropped to the deck near the right-side gangway. He could see partway up into the rocks where the *banditos* were; their cover was good and the angle made shooting difficult from down here. But their angle, shooting downward, was much better. Their bullets spanged off the steel-plated sides of the locomotive, ricocheted with echoing howls through the mountain vastness.

The posse had recovered from the sudden braking and were once again firing through the car's windows, forcing the raiders to remain where they were in the rocks flanking both sides of the tracks. From his position near the gangway, M'Candliss squeezed off twice at a bearded face that appeared from behind one of the crags. Both shots, hurried as they were, missed low and sent showers of rock dust into the *bandito*'s face.

M'Candliss ducked back, crawled across to where his rifle was wedged next to the fireman's seat. At the left-side gangway, the fireman was crouched with his head down, cursing a blue streak and firing his revolver sporadically around the steel side guard. Frederickson, despite the pain of his wounded shoulder, was hunkered alongside him; he had a smoking pistol in his hand as well.

Coming back with his rifle, M'Candliss waited until the bearded outlaw showed himself again. Then he raised up and snapped off a quick shot, and this time he didn't miss. His bullet took the man in the throat, brought him toppling out of the rocks to sprawl along the right-of-way.

The rest of the *banditos* continued to pour lead down from above, pinning M'Candliss and the posse inside the train. There was no way for any of them to get out without being cut down by the crossfire of fifty guns. They seemed to be trapped there, helpless, with no way of warning or stopping the approaching delegates' special. And once that special reached the trestle over the chasm, and began to cross it . . .

M'Candliss emptied his rifle at the rocks, hunkered low to reload. The heavy continuous gunfire filled the early morning with hollow reverberations of sound. The sun was rising, still hidden behind the peaks but showing an aureole of radiance at their tips. M'Candliss glanced up there and then hauled out his stemwinder again. Close to eight-thirty —

And suddenly, above the hammering of rifles and revolvers, he heard the low mournful wail of a train whistle. It could only be the delegates' train, a half-hour early and starting up the grade on the opposite side of the gorge.

Damn! A coldness gripped him as he listened to the whistle blow a second time; from its clarity, he judged that the train was no more than a mile from the chasm now — a mile from death for all those on board. They wouldn't hear the gunfire until it was too late for the engineer to stop. And there was nothing M'Candliss or the posse could do, pinned down the way they were . . .

M'Candliss' mind whirled, spun up an idea. It was close to suicidal as far as his own hide was concerned, but if Providence was still looking their way he might be able to save the lives of the American officials on that special. But he had to act immediately; there was no time for weighing and considering, only time for action.

He turned his head, shouted across the cab to Frederickson and the fireman, "Start shoveling coal into the firebox! Get the pressure up on those gauges again!"

Frederickson looked across at him as if he had gone loco. "What the hell for?"

"Don't you hear that whistle? That's the dele-gates' train! The only way to stop it is to blow up the trestle *before they reach it.* They'll hear the ex-plosion and maybe they'll be able to stop in time."

"God Almighty!" Frederickson exclaimed. "You ain't fixin' to run this hog out onto that trestle yourself, are you?"

"That's just what I'm fixing to do," M'Candliss answered tensely. "There's no other way."

The wounded engineer and the fireman were staring at him with a mixture of respect and plain awe; neither of them moved for two or three seconds. Then the fireman snapped, "All right, then! Give me that shovel, Fred. M'Candliss wants steam pressure, by God he'll get steam pressure!"

M'Candliss waited until there was a break in the shooting, then shoved up and ran onto the footplate in front of the tender. He crouched there, protected by the side guard, and yelled at the top of his voice, "Tucker! Ed Tucker! Open the door so I can talk to you!"

Moments later there was an answering bellow from the passenger car. "Tucker here!" He was also answered by a volley of shots from the surrounding rocks; bullets whined off metal, burrowed through the coal.

"I'm here, Oak!" Tucker shouted again.

"I'm going to uncouple us," M'Candliss called back. "I'll need cover fire."

"Why? What's the idea?"

"No time for explanations. I need that cover!"

"All right, Cap, you've got it!" It was Meckleburg who shouted that; he must have been close to the sheriff at the open door. Then both men turned back inside because seconds later M'Candliss could hear them instructing the rest of the posse to step up their firing.

As soon as the rifles and pistols were creating a simultaneous roar from inside the car, M'Candliss took a deep breath and then pushed up and scrambled across the coal in the tender. His boots struck the metal of the platform beyond, and he dropped to his knees at the pincoupler which joined the locomotive to the car. Feverishly, he dug at the fastenings of the pin, loosening it, trying to pull it free. Two slugs whined off the tender, a third cut an angry path past his bowed head, narrowly missing. His fingers were broken-nailed and bleeding, but he paid them no mind. He could still hear, above the din, the mournful wail of the whistle on the delegates' train.

Another bullet hummed by, and there were shouts from the men inside the passenger car as they sent round after round of lead at the *banditos* in the rocks. Behind M'Candliss, in the locomotive's cab, he could hear the fireman cursing vehemently as he fed coal to the boiler, and Frederickson's shouts that the steam pressure was beginning to rise.

After what seemed like minutes, M'Candliss managed to work the pin free of the couplers. He flung it down, pivoted upward, and rolled back across the coal into the cab of the locomotive. Lumps of sooty anthracite bounced out with him, clattering on the footboards; a slug plucked at his forearm, stinging, but he scarcely felt it. He went to where Frederickson crouched at the controls.

"I thought you were a goner out there for sure,

Mister," the old engineer said.

M'Candliss grunted, staring at the gauges. "Have we got enough pressure yet?"

"She'll move, but she won't break any speed records."

Before M'Candliss could respond, the whistle on the delegates' special sounded again. If his judgement was correct, it was less than a half-mile from the gorge now and climbing fast. Time was running out.

He snapped, "You boys had better jump for the car — now! I'll take it from here."

Both Frederickson and the fireman hesitated, but the authority and urgency in M'Candliss' voice decided them. Helping the wounded engineer onto the footplate, the fireman shouted to Tucker to open the car door — they were coming across. M'Candliss heard the sheriff's answering shout, saw Frederickson and the sooty fireman go scrambling over the coal and down onto the platform. The men of the posse covered them with another fusillade as they dodged safely inside.

M'Candliss was already at the controls. He released the brakes, pulled the throttle open. The ancient locomotive began to edge forward, drivers clanking as they turned, steam hissing loudly inside the boiler. More bullets whanged off its metal hide as Gueterma and his *banditos* realized what was happening, but M'Candliss kept his head down below the side window as he worked the throttle and checked the gauges.

The 4-4-0 seemed to inch along as if it were a

gigantic black slug, even though he had the throttle wide open. The stuttering clamor of the valves and the staccato beat of the exhaust swelled against his ears, but the needle on the pressure gauge wavered low. There simply hadn't been enough time to build up enough pressure for any kind of speed.

The whistles on the Prescott train sounded again from across the gorge, much louder now, echoing in M'Candliss' mind with the continual reminder that time was fast running out. He poked his head outside for an instant, risking a bullet, as slugs screamed off the locomotive's sides. The cowcatcher had almost reached the trestle.

He could see the sheer rock walls of Saddleback Gorge, the dizzying drop to the rocks below, and he knew that if he didn't want that to be his final resting place, he had to jump soon. But if he left the throttle, it would close automatically and the locomotive would stop before it reached the place where the raiders had rigged out their dynamite. Frantic-eyed, he looked around the cab for some way to hold the throttle wide open.

Then he saw the coal shovel which the fireman had dropped just before he and Frederickson had jumped for the passenger car. He bent, picked it up. Working rapidly, he managed to jam the tool between the throttle and the side guard, wedging it in as tight as his straining muscles would allow. If he jumped, and it popped loose . . .

M'Candliss refused to think about that. The

shovel would hold. It *had* to hold. He turned from the controls and ran to the gangway, keeping low. He poised there as the locomotive nosed out onto the trestle.

And then he lept out to the side, away from the gorge but onto unprotected open ground — straight into the murderous fire from Gueterma's *banditos* in the rocks above.

FOURTEEN

M'Candliss landed on his feet, staggered forward several steps in an upright position, and then sprawled onto the rocky ground with jarring impact. Bullets gouged the earth around him as he rolled toward a melon-shaped boulder set almost but not quite flush against the cliff. Miraculously, he reached the safety of the natural shield unhurt.

He came up next to the boulder with the .44 still clenched in his right hand, having held it in close to his body with his finger clear of the trigger when he jumped from the locomotive. He pitched his body into the narrow space between the boulder and the wall, conscious of stinging pain in his arms and legs from rock cuts during his fall and roll. More whistling lead chipped splinters from the stone behind him.

He saw that the 4-4-0 was full on the trestle now, still seeming to crawl snail-like along the steel rails and wooden struts. The shovel was holding. He moved his gaze back to where the passenger car sat by itself some fifty yards from the trestle. The men from Adobe Junction were

165

still sending heavy fire at the renegades, keeping them pretty well pinned down in their entrenchment. It was this relentless firepower which had allowed M'Candliss to escape unharmed from the locomotive.

He sent two shots from his own weapon winging across at a raider who tried to move from one outcropping to another; the man twisted, fell from view. Seconds later M'Candliss heard the keening moan of the approaching train once more, so close that he knew it was just beyond the corner of the opposite ridge. As he peered across the chasm, he saw the advancing plume of smoke from its stack drifting up over the rocks. Any second now the special's locomotive would steam into view.

Heart hammering, M'Candliss brought his eyes back to the 4-4-0 on the trestle — just in time to see the explosion.

There was an ear-splitting concussion, a blinding flash of orange light and acrid black smoke. Flying bridge particles and locomotive sections erupted through the flame and smoke; metal splinters and lumps of coal rained down all around. Some struck the unprotected *banditos* in the rocks; M'Candliss heard shouts and short, terrified screams.

The fireball that engulfed the locomotive licked hungrily at the broken, teetering wreck that had once been the trestle. Then M'Candliss, safe in his niche behind the boulder, saw what was left of the old engine fall end over end with a trail of fire toward the rock-strewn bottom of the gorge.

As the last rumble of the explosion died away, there came the sound of two long whistle blasts from the delegates' train. Then its locomotive hove into view around the far bend, sparks flying from its wheel flanges as the engineer, having heard the explosion and able now to see what had happened to the trestle, applied full brakes. The cars behind swayed violently; the tortured scream of locking brake shoes and metal grinding on metal reverberated off the cliff walls.

More of the burning trestle crumbled and followed the debris into the chasm; the last remaining timbers were disintegrating, like an arch with its capstone missing will collapse. The oncoming locomotive skidded toward the brink, and for an instant M'Candliss thought it would slide off the twisted rails at the edge and plunge downward, carrying its string of cars with it.

But then he saw it shudder, like a huge animal shaking itself, and come to a rattling stop no more than a dozen yards from the gorge. Relief surged inside him as he watched smoke belch from the locomotive's stack, blanket the cars behind in sooty plumes. There was a rocking jerk, and then the engine, a big Mallett-Hubbard, slowly reversed from the gaping maw.

In the ranks of the outlaws, mass confusion seemed to have taken over. They were no longer shooting at the Adobe Junction posse, and Meckleburg, Tucker, and the others, sensing that the tide of battle had turned in their favor, burst from the car with their weapons blazing. A half dozen of the *banditos* spilled dead or wounded from their positions above, and the others suddenly seemed loath to stand and fight; there was only sporadic answering fire. The possemen, fanning out on both sides of the tracks, made it to cover without losing a single one of their number.

High in the rocks directly across the right-of-way came a sudden angry bellow. M'Candliss, reloading his pistol, recognized the voice as Frederico Gueterma's — a voice maddened with rage and frustration.

"Attack!" Gueterma was screaming at his renegades. "Run the *anglos* into the gorge! We still outnumber them, you fools! *Fusilar! Fusilar!*"

The outlaws responded sluggishly, as if they knew the cause was now futile. Some showed themselves, only to be cut down by the bullets of the possemen. Now it was the *anglos,* the honest men of Arizona, who were on the offensive. And it was plain that they could taste the sweetness of victory and revenge.

The *banditos* floundered. Then, in a body, those still alive fled in headlong retreat, disobeying their *grande general* as they ran for their horses and their lives. The men from Adobe Junction cut down more of the fleeing raiders, showing them the same lack of quarter that they had shown the people of the villages they had pillaged and destroyed.

M'Candliss left his niche behind the boulder and the possemen swarmed from their concealment, giving chase among the outcroppings on both sides of the tracks. None of the outlaws stood to face the onrushing men. M'Candliss ran across the right-of-way, up into the rocks toward the place where he had heard Gueterma yelling. When he and some of the men from Adobe Junction crested the ridge on that side he saw that several of the *banditos* had gathered their horses and were scattering down a narrow twisting trail. But Gueterma wasn't one of them.

The possemen gave chase down the trail. M'Candliss turned the other way, sharp-eyed and watchful, to search through the rocks and jackpine strewn along the ridge.

"You!"

M'Candliss whirled at the sudden outcry, dropping to one knee. The muzzle flash of a pistol came from a jagged series of rocks on his immediate left; he felt the searing heat of a bullet pass along his right cheek, almost burning the skin. Then Gueterma appeared, a pearl-handled revolver in his right hand, his eyes wild with hatred. He fired again, but M'Candliss threw himself to the left and the bullet missed harmlessly.

Before Gueterma could line up for a third shot, M'Candliss flattened out on his belly and triggered his .44. The bullet sent the pearl-handled *pistola* flying and brought a howl of pain from Gueterma.

M'Candliss shoved up to one knee, then onto his feet, keeping the .44 leveled. The Mexican stood clutching at his wounded hand, glaring with more malevolence than M'Candliss had ever seen in one man's eyes.

"You *demonio!*" Gueterma screamed at him. "You are not a mere man to have escaped death at the hands of fifty! You alone did this! You alone prevented my plan from succeeding!"

"Not just me, Gueterma," M'Candliss said. "Isabella Ortiz, a dozen hard men from Adobe Junction, and a handful of others too."

"No, it was *you!* I would have become *El Presidente* but for you!"

"You'd never have become *El Presidente,*" M'Candliss told him. "Not as long as your country and mine are full of decent people. You could have had an army, Gueterma, and you still wouldn't have got what you wanted."

"What I had were pigs, deserting me, betraying me. If only I had had you or a dozen like you!" His mouth twisted bitterly. "Instead of killing you, or threatening to kill you, I should have bought your services."

"Your kind can never buy me."

"I would have given you gold, a fortune in gold —"

"There's not enough gold in Arizona to put me on your side of the fence."

"You mock me, *Capitan.*"

"Maybe so. I'm sick of the sight of you."

The wildness blazed brighter in the Mexican's eyes. "I will kill you!" he bellowed, "I will grind your bones into powder and spit on what is left!"

"Your killing days are over, Gueterma —"

170

With the suddenness of a rattler uncoiling, Gueterma launched himself at M'Candliss. The ranger sidestepped, fired a warning shot, but Gueterma kept coming, bull-like, head down and arms outstretched. M'Candliss triggered another shot, not as a warning this time, trying to bring the Mexican down, but his aim was hurried; the bullet missed wide. Then Gueterma was on him, swinging viciously. One flailing arm struck M'Candliss' wrist and dislodged the .44, sent it clattering against an outcropping. Another wild punch slammed into M'Candliss' cheekbone, made his head rock and sing with the impact. He staggered back, managed to gain leverage, then drove his fist into Gueterma's stomach. But the blow barely fazed Gueterma. It brought a grunt and an even more savage assault. Bloodlust had consumed the man — a crazed need to kill the one person he held responsible for destroying his fanatical plot.

But there was rage in M'Candliss too, and an urge to vent it on this hellborn traitor. He blocked most of Gueterma's swings and landed a few of his own. The two men fought toe to toe, like bare-knuckled prizefighters, each of them hurt but neither of them yielding, both driven by the frenzy of their feelings.

It might have gone on like that for minutes, except that M'Candliss' foot slipped, throwing him momentarily off balance, and one of Gueterma's punches hammered through his guard. The blow took him on the temple; a reddish haze seemed to erupt behind his eyes, blurring his vision. He stumbled, and before he could regain his balance, Gueterma hit him twice more in the face and knocked him sprawling.

Dazed, M'Candliss pawed at his eyes and shook his head. When his eyes focused again he saw that Gueterma had wheeled and was scooping up his pearl-handled *pistola*. He scrambled to his feet just as the Mexican, lips peeled in against his teeth, swung around with the pistol; and M'Candliss knew he wouldn't be able to reach the man before he fired —

A shot cracked out.

But it did not come from the weapon in Gueterma's hand; it came from somewhere behind M'Candliss. And for the second time he saw the pearl-handled revolver jump loose, heard Gueterma let out a cry of pain. M'Candliss swiveled his head, looked behind him.

Meckleburg and Sheriff Tucker were standing there, and Meckleburg had his rifle leveled and a tight grin on his face. "That makes it a fair fight again," he called. "Go on, Cap — finish him off."

M'Candliss jerked his hand in thanks, turned to face Gueterma again as the Mexican charged. As soon as they came together, M'Candliss stabbed a sharp right into Gueterma's ribcage; followed it with a left under the wishbone. Gueterma staggered, air spewing from his mouth, his eyes glazing. M'Candliss went after him, slid under a wild retaliatory swing, and broke Gueterma's nose with a hard right fist. Blood sprayed over both of them, rivuleted down over the Mexican's Van Dyke beard. Gueterma skidded backward, wobbled, and sprawled on the ground.

But he wasn't finished yet; he struggled to rise. M'Candliss threw himself on the man, straddled him, and put everything he had left into a sweeping right cross that landed on the point of Gueterma's bloody beard.

A bone cracked. Gueterma screamed like a woman, and then the fire went out of his eyes and they clouded over. He lay still, breathing stertorously, blood still leaking from his smashed nose.

M'Candliss got slowly and painfully to his feet. He stood over the unconscious Mexican for several seconds, dragging in deep lungfuls of the hot mountain air. Then, at last, he turned away and went to where Meckleburg and Tucker waited. Inside him now was a kind of peace, born of the knowledge that this battle had been won and that the people of Arizona would suffer no more at the hands of Frederico Gueterma and his *bandito* horde.

FIFTEEN

With the outlaws vanquished, their Galiuro fortress overrun by two companies of Territorial Rangers, and their leader in a well-guarded cell in the Territorial prison at Yuma awaiting extradition to Mexico, the international conference in Prescott was almost an anticlimax. But it was the kind of anticlimax M'Candliss was proud to be a part of, and that he would have liked to see happen more often.

The U.S. and Mexican delegates arrived a couple of days after the fight at Saddleback Gorge, a little worse for wear but exceedingly pleased that their mission was no longer such a grim one. Their train had had to reverse all the way to Lordsburg, then re-route along a northern spur and drop down to Prescott via the Painted Desert and Flagstaff. After General Porfirio Diaz learned what had happened via telegraph, he sent another emissary immediately. Governor Shannon and Clement Holmes, who had recovered from his grippe without any serious complications, were never more pontifical. And the meeting became a good-will exchange which did much to further the closeness of the two countries.

M'Candliss was lauded for his bravery, as were Meckleburg and Tucker and the posse from Adobe Junction. Flynn, who was also present, having gone to Prescott from the raid on the *bandito* fortress, also came in for his share of praise. But he was mightily disappointed that he hadn't been able to take part in the skirmish at Saddleback Gorge, and vowed that the next time there was a fight, he intended to be right in the middle of it, come hell or high water.

Isabella Ortiz was there as well. Despite her earlier avowal to unseat Diaz, no animosity was shown by either her or the new emissary from Mexico City. An unwritten truce had been posted, although M'Candliss knew that she would continue to do everything in her power to see that her people's lot was bettered — through peaceful means.

As for Ramon Esteban, whose *revolucionarios* still roamed the Mexican state of Chihuahua, the subject was not discussed at the conference. Esteban, as long as he remained on his own side of the border, was no concern of the United States. By tacit agreement, it was accepted that the internal problems of Mexico would be dealt with without outside interference.

On the last night of the conference, there was a farewell party — a final gathering of dignitaries and concerned individuals who would be returning to their various homes in the two nations come morning. The celebration lasted far into the night, with Governor Shannon giving a speech that had only been out-oratoried by his inaugural address, and the Mexican emissary following with one of similar eloquence, before the participants devoted themselves to food and liquor, music and dancing.

The party was the first opportunity M'Candliss had to speak to Isabella privately; the conference had kept them both too busy for socializing. They ate together, danced together, and later on they slipped out and went for a walk together in the moonlight.

"What will you do now, Isabella?" he asked her, even though he knew the answer. "Will you return to Mexico?"

"Yes, I must," she said. "I must do whatever I can to help my people."

"By rejoining Esteban and his guerillas?"

She was silent for a time. "I do not know, *Capitan*," she said gravely. "Perhaps. Perhaps not."

"You saw how much was accomplished at the conference. There's more to be gained at the bargaining table than with guns."

"Once I would have scorned such an idea."

"And now?"

"I am willing to consider it."

"Good. I think you'll make the right decision, Isabella."

"I can only hope that God grants me the wisdom."

They walked in silence for a time. M'Candliss

was acutely aware of her beauty — *hers*, not the similarities to Rachel's — and inside him there was a small, dull ache of loneliness. That ache had been there ever since the death of his wife, and perhaps it would always be there, because there were few women whom he could love and who could love him. His wife had been one. And Isabella Ortiz, perhaps, was another. But they were of different worlds, if not of different ideals. In another time, another place, they might have courted and been married and produced fine children. That time was not now — but it might come some day.

He said these things to her later, after he had walked her back to her hotel. He said them on impulse, and felt foolish afterward, but Isabella seemed moved by them, as if similar thoughts had been on her own mind. Her eyes were soft as she looked at him, and she touched his cheek with gentle fingers.

"Yes," she said, "perhaps some day, my *Capitan*. It is something for both of us to dream about, *verdad?*"

He nodded. "Something to dream about," he said.

Her eyes probed his for a long moment. Then she stepped close and kissed him — one of the sweetest kisses M'Candliss had ever known.

"*Vaya con Dios*," she said then.

"You too. Go with God, Isabella."

She smiled, touched his cheek again. "*Hasta luego, mi Capitan*," she said softly, and a moment later she was gone inside her room.

"Till we meet again," M'Candliss murmured. And he knew that they would meet again, some day, and that that meeting would be a momentous one for both of them.

If people dreamed long enough and hard enough about such things as peace and freedom and love, their dreams were bound to come true . . .

The employees of G.K. Hall hope you have enjoyed this Large Print book. All our Large Print titles are designed for easy reading, and all our books are made to last. Other G.K. Hall books are available at your library, through selected bookstores, or directly from us.

For information about titles, please call:

(800) 223-1244
(800) 223-6121

To share your comments, please write:

Publisher
G.K. Hall & Co.
295 Kennedy Memorial Drive
Waterville, ME 04901